SECRET HARBOUR

The *Comte* kissed her until she felt that she was no longer herself but utterly and completely his. He raised his head to say in a voice that was unsteady: "My darling, I did not mean this to happen."

"I love . . . you!" Grania said. "I . . . thought I had . . . lost you."

"You will never do that as long as I am alive, *ma cherie*."

"You . . . love me?"

"Of course I love you!" he said almost angrily. "But it is something I should not do any more than you should love me."

"How can I help it?" Grania asked.

Then he was kissing her again, kissing her until she felt as if he carried l̶ ̶ ̶ ̶ ̶ ̶ ̶ ̶ ̶d there were no ̶ ̶ ̶ ̶ ̶ ̶ ̶ ̶ ̶ ̶ng but themselve̶ ̶

Bantam Books by Barbara Cartland
Ask your bookseller for the books you have missed

Barbara Cartland's Library of Love Series
THE OBSTACLE RACE

About Barbara Cartland
CRUSADER IN PINK

Secret Harbour

Barbara Cartland

BANTAM BOOKS
TORONTO · NEW YORK · LONDON · SYDNEY

SECRET HARBOUR

A Bantam Book / January 1982

ISBN 0-553-20505-6

Published simultaneously in the United States and Canada

Bantam Books are published by Bantam Books, Inc. Its trade-
mark, consisting of the words ''Bantam Books'' and the por-
trayal of a rooster, is Registered in U.S. Patent and Trademark
Office and in other countries. Marca Registrada. Bantam
Books, Inc., 666 Fifth Avenue, New York, New York 10103.

PRINTED IN THE UNITED STATES OF AMERICA

0 9 8 7 6 5 4 3 2 1

Author's Note

The slaves' revolution in Grenada under Julius Fédor ended in April 1796. In the Parish of St. George's there was no fighting.

Martinique, which was first colonised by the French in 1635, was recaptured from the British in 1802.

I visited Martinique in 1976 and found it fascinating, with every good French characteristic including delicious food. I wrote a novel about it called *The Magic of Love*.

In 1981 I paid my first visit to Grenada. "The Isle of Spice" is as lovely as the guide books describe it, and although in 1980 it became a Communist state, the only signs of it were the large posters exhorting the population to support the revolution. This I learnt had been completely bloodless, and the charming, smiling Grenadians are delighted to welcome visitors.

The tropical forests, the golden beaches, and the plantations of nutmegs, cocoa beans, and bananas are all as I have described them in this novel.

The sun shines, the shrubs are vivid patches of brilliant colour, and the palm trees wave in the breeze from a blue and emerald sea.

What more could we ask?

Chapter One

1795

Grania walked quickly up the stairs and stood at the top listening.

The house was dark, but it was not only the darkness that made her feel frightened.

She was frightened as she listened to the voices coming from the Dining-Room, and frightened by an atmosphere that she sensed was tense, if not evil.

In the last month she had been looking forward with an almost childish excitement to being back in Grenada, feeling that she was coming home and that everything would be as it had been three years ago when she had left.

Instead of which, once they had reached the green islands which had always seemed to her to resemble emeralds set in a sea of blue, everything began to go wrong.

When her father had said he was taking her home, she had been so sure that she would be happy again with the same happiness which had been hers in the years when she had lived in what had always seemed a magical island.

It had been inhabited not only by smiling people but also, she felt, by gods and goddesses who dwelt on the tops of the mountains, and fairies and gnomes who

1

moved so swiftly amongst the nutmeg and cocoa trees that she had only a fleeting glimpse of them.

"It will be so exciting to be back at Secret Harbour," Grania had said to her father when they had passed through the storms of the Atlantic.

The sea was smooth and clear and glittered in the sunshine, and the sailors as they climbed the masts sang songs that Grania remembered were part of her childhood.

Her father did not answer, and after a moment she looked at him questioningly.

"Is something worrying you, Papa?"

He had not been drinking as much during the last few days as he had at the beginning of the voyage, and despite what her mother had called his "dissipated life," he still looked amazingly handsome.

"I want to talk to you sometime, Grania," he replied, "about your future."

"My future, Papa?"

Her father did not answer, and after a moment she said, as a sudden fear struck her like a streak of lightning:

"What are you ... saying? My future is with ... you. I am going to ... look after you as Mama did ... and I am sure we will be very happy ... together."

"I have different plans for you."

Grania stared at him incredulously.

Then one of the Officers of the ship had come up to speak to them and her father moved away from her in a way which told her that he had no wish to continue the conversation.

What he meant and what he had intended to say worried her all through the day.

She had wanted to discuss it with him later in the evening, but they had dined with the Captain and after dinner her father was incapable of having a coherent conversation with anybody.

It was the same the next day and the next, and only when the ship was actually within sight of the high mountains that she knew so well did Grania manage to find her father alone at the ship's rail and say to him insistently:

"You must tell me, Papa, what you are planning before we reach home."

"We are not going straight home," the Earl of Kilkerry replied.

"Not going home?"

"No. I have arranged that we shall stay for a night or two with Roderick Maigrin."

"Why?"

The question was sharp and seemed almost to burst from Grania's lips.

"He wants to see you, Grania—in fact he is very anxious to do so."

"Why?" Grania asked again, and now the sound that came from her seemed to tremble on the air.

She felt as if her father braced himself before he answered. Then he said in a gruff tone which told her he was embarrassed:

"You are eighteen. It is time you were married."

For a moment it was impossible for Grania to reply; impossible even to draw in her breath.

Then she said in a voice which did not sound like her own:

"Are you . . . saying, Papa . . . that Mr. Maigrin . . . wishes to . . . marry me?"

Even as she asked the question she thought it was too incredible even to contemplate.

She remembered Roderick Maigrin. He was a neighbour of whom her mother had never approved and whom she had always discouraged from visiting Secret Harbour.

A thick-set, hard-drinking, rough-speaking man who was suspected, Grania remembered, of being a cruel task-master on his plantation.

He was old, almost as old as her father, and to think of marrying him was so absurd that if she had not been frightened she would have laughed at the very idea.

"Maigrin is a good chap," her father was saying, "and a very rich one."

That was not the whole answer, Grania thought later.

Roderick Maigrin was rich, and her father as usual was in a state of penury and had to rely on the generosity of his friends even for the rum he drank.

It was her father's propensity for drinking, gambling, and neglecting his plantations which had made her mother run away three years earlier.

"What hope have you, darling, of getting any education in this place?" she had said to her daughter. "We see nobody but those dissolute friends of your father's who encourage him to drink and gamble away on the cards every penny of his income!"

"Papa is always sorry that he makes you angry, Mama," Grania had replied.

For a moment her mother's eyes had softened. Then she had said:

"Yes, he is sorry, and I have forgiven him and gone on forgiving him. But now I have to think about you."

Grania had not understood, and her mother had continued:

"You are very lovely, my darling, and it is only right that you should have the chance that I had of meeting your social equals and going to the Balls and parties to which your position entitles you."

Again Grania had not understood, for there were no parties in Grenada unless her father and mother went to stay with friends at St. George's or Charlotte Town.

But she was very happy at Secret Harbour, playing with the children of the slaves, although those of her own age were already working.

Almost before she realised what was happening, her mother had taken her away, leaving very early one morning while her father was still sleeping off the excesses of the night before.

In the beautiful harbour of St. George's overlooked by the Fort there was a large ship, and almost as soon as they were aboard, it moved out into the open sea and away from the island that had been her home ever since she had been six years old.

It was only when they reached London and her

mother got in touch with several old friends that Grania learnt how adventurous her mother had been in marrying the handsome Earl of Kilkerry when she was only eighteen, and six years later going out with him to start a strange new life on an island in the Caribbean.

"Your mother was so beautiful," one of her mother's friends had said to Grania, "and when she left us we felt as if London lost a shining jewel. Now she is back to shine as she did in the old days, and we are very thrilled to see her again."

But things were not the same, Grania soon learnt, because her mother's father was now dead, her other relations had grown old and no longer lived in London, and they had not enough money to make a mark in the gay social life which centred round the young Prince of Wales.

The Countess of Kilkerry, however, made her curtsey to the King and Queen and promised that as soon as Grania was old enough she should do the same.

"In the meantime, my dearest," she said, "you will have to work hard to catch up with all the education you have missed."

Grania did in fact work very hard, because she wanted to please her mother and she also wanted to learn.

There was a School she attended daily, and there were extra teachers who came to the small house her mother had rented in Mayfair.

There was little time for anything but her lessons, but she did realise that her mother had a number of friends whom she was continually visiting for luncheon and dinner and who took her to the Italian Opera House and Vauxhall Gardens.

It seemed to Grania that without the insistent worry over her father's drinking and gaming, her mother looked very much younger and certainly more beautiful.

Besides which, the new gowns she had bought immediately on reaching London were very becoming.

The full muslin skirts, the satin sashes, and the fichus

which framed her mother's shoulders were very different from the gowns they had made for themselves in Grenada.

There was little choice of material in St. George's, and Grania had worn the same bright, coarse cottons which were the pride and joy of the native women.

In London she developed her taste not only for gowns but for furniture, paintings, and people.

Then, when she was nearly eighteen and her mother was planning to present her to the King and Queen, the Countess became ill.

Perhaps it was the fogs and the cold of winter that she felt more acutely than her friends because she had lived in a warm climate for so long, or perhaps it was the treacherous fevers which were always prevalent in London.

Whatever it was, the Countess grew weaker and weaker until despairingly she said to Grania:

"I think you should write to your father and ask him to come to us at once. There must be somebody to look after you if I die."

Grania gave a cry of horror.

"Do not think of dying, Mama! You will get better as soon as the winter is over. It is only the cold which makes you cough and feel so ill."

But her mother had insisted, and because she felt it was only right that her father should know how ill she was, Grania had written to him.

She was well aware that it would take some time for her letter to be answered, just as during the years they had been away they had heard from him only sporadically.

Sometimes letters must have been lost at sea, but others arrived which were long and full of information about the house, the plantations, the prices he had got for the nutmeg crop or the cocoa beans, and whether it was a good season for bananas.

At other times, after months, there would be just a scrawl, written with a hand that was too unsteady to hold the pen.

When these letters came, Grania knew by the way

her mother's lips tightened and the expression on her face that she was thinking how right she had been to come away.

She knew that if they had been at home there would have been the same repeated scenes over her father's drinking, the same apologies, and the same acts of forgiveness after the reiteration of the same promises he would not keep.

Once Grania had said to her mother:

"As we are spending your money, Mama, here in England, how is Papa managing at home?"

For a moment she had thought her mother would not answer. Then the Countess had replied:

"What little money I have is now being spent on you, Grania. Your father must learn to stand on his own feet. It will be the best thing that could happen if he learns to depend on himself rather than on me."

Grania had not said anything, but she had a feeling that her father would always find somebody on whom he could depend, and if it was not her mother it would be one of his friends who drank and gambled with him.

However badly he behaved, however much he drank, however much her mother complained of his neglect of his property and of her, the Earl had an Irish charm and fascination that everybody who knew him found hard to resist.

Grania knew that when he was not drinking he was more fun to be with and a more exciting companion than anybody she had ever known.

It was his laughter that was infectious, and the way he could find a story and a joke in everything.

"Give your father two potatoes and a wooden box, and he will mesmerise you into believing it is a carriage and pair that will carry you to a King's Palace!" one of her father's friends had said to Grania when she was a little girl, and she had never forgotten.

It was true.

Her father found life an amusing adventure which he could never take seriously, and it was difficult for any-body who was in his company to think otherwise.

But now Grania knew that the three years they had been apart had changed him.

He could still laugh, could still make the tales he told have a magical quality about them that was irresistible, but at the same time she had known all the way across the Atlantic that he was keeping something from her, and when they actually arrived at Grenada she learnt what it was.

She had taken it for granted that after the tragedy of her mother's death he would want her to be with him and try to create a happy home together.

Instead, incredibly, he wished to marry her off to a man whom she had disliked when she was a child and knew that her mother had despised.

The ship in which they were travelling, which was to dock in the harbour at St. George's, had in the obliging manner which was usual in the Caribbean sailed a little way off course to set them down where her father wished.

Roderick Maigrin's plantation was in the adjoining Parish to St. George's, which had been named by the British "St. David."

It was the only Parish on the island without a town and was in the south of the island adjoining St. George's, and it was very similar in respect of the beauty of its landscape and the people who lived there.

At Westerhall Point, which was a small peninsula covered with flowering trees and shrubs, Roderick Maigrin had built himself a large house that was somewhat pretentious in aspect, and to Grania it had all the characteristics of its owner, so that instinctively she disliked it.

She could never remember visiting it as a child, but now as they were rowed ashore in Mr. Maigrin's boat which had come out to the ship to collect them, she had the terrifying feeling that she was entering a prison.

It would be impossible for her to escape, and she would no longer be herself but entirely subservient to the large, red-faced man who was waiting to greet them.

"Glad to see you back, Kilkerry!" Roderick Maigrin shouted in a loud, over-hearty voice, clapping the Earl on the back.

Then as he stretched out his hand towards Grania and she saw the expression in his eyes, it was only with a tremendous effort of will that she did not run frantically back towards the ship.

But it was already sailing westwards to round the point of the island before it turned north to reach St. George's harbour.

Roderick Maigrin led them inside the house to where a servant was already preparing rum punches in long glasses.

There was a gleam in the Earl's eye as he lifted his glass to his lips.

"I have been waiting for this moment ever since I left England," he said.

Roderick Maigrin laughed.

"That is what I thought you would say," he said. "So drink up! There is plenty more where that came from, and I want to drink the health of the lovely girl you have brought back with you."

He raised his glass as he spoke, and Grania thought that his blood-shot eyes leered at her as if he was mentally undressing her.

She hated him so violently that she knew she could not stay in the same room without telling him so.

She made the excuse that she wished to retire to her bedroom, but when a servant told her what time dinner was served she was forced to wash and change and go downstairs, making herself behave as her mother would have expected, with dignity.

As she had anticipated, by this time her father had already had a great deal of drink and so had their host.

Grania was aware not only that the rum punches were strong but that their action was accumulative.

By the end of the dinner neither man made any pretence of eating; they were only drinking, toasting each other and her, and making it quite clear that she was to be married as soon as the ceremony could be arranged.

What was so insulting to Grania was that Roderick Maigrin had not even paid her the lip-service of asking her to be his wife but had taken it for granted.

She had already learnt in London that a daughter was not expected to question the arrangements her parents made on her behalf when it came to marriage.

At first she wondered how her father could think that a coarse, elderly, hard-drinking man like Roderick Maigrin would be a suitable husband for her.

Then what they said to each other and the innuendoes in Roderick Maigrin's remarks made Grania sure that he was paying her father for the privilege of becoming her husband, and her father was well satisfied with the deal.

As course succeeded course, she sat at the dining-table not speaking but only listening with horror to the two men who were treating her as if she were a puppet with no feelings, no sensitivity, and certainly no opinions of her own.

She was to be married whether she liked it or not, and she would become the property of a man she loathed, a property as completely as were any of the slaves who lived and breathed only because he allowed them to.

She disliked everything he said and the way he said it.

"Any excitements while I have been away?" her father asked.

"That cursed pirate Will Wilken came in the night, took six of my best pigs and a dozen turkeys, and slit the throat of the boy who tried to stop him."

"It was brave of the lad not to run away," the Earl remarked.

"He was a blasted fool, if you ask me, to take on Wilken single-handed," Roderick Maigrin replied.

"Anything else?"

"There's another damned pirate, a Frenchman, scudding

about, called Beaufort. If I see him, I'll blow a piece of lead between his eyes."

Grania was only half-listening, and not until the meal had ended and the servants put a number of bottles on the table before they filled up the glasses and left the room did she realise she could escape.

She was quite certain that her father, at any rate, was past noticing whether she was there or not, and she thought that Roderick Maigrin, drinking with him, would find it difficult if he tried to follow her.

She therefore waited until she was sure they had for the moment forgotten her existence, then quickly and without speaking she slipped from the room, closing the door behind her.

Then as she went up the stairs to the only place in which she felt assured of any privacy, she wondered what she could do.

Trembling, she was frantically trying to think if there was anybody on the island to whom she could go for help.

Then she knew that even if they were prepared to assist her, her father could collect her without their being able to prevent it or even to protest.

As she stood on the landing trying to consider what she should do, she heard Roderick Maigrin laugh, and it sounded like the last horror to impinge upon her consciousness and make her realise how helpless she was.

She felt that it was the laugh of a man who had not only drunk too much but who was pleased and satisfied with his lot, a man who had got what he desired.

Then, almost as if somebody were explaining it to her in words, Grania knew the answer.

Roderick Maigrin wanted her not only for her looks— and that was obvious from the expression in his eyes— but also because she was her father's daughter and therefore socially of some importance even in the small community that existed on Grenada.

She thought it was the reason why he had been

attracted to her father in the first place, not only
because they were neighbours but because he wanted
to be a friend of the man who was received, consulted,
and respected by the Governor and everybody else who
mattered.

Before she had left the island Grania had begun to
understand the social snobbishness which existed wherever the British ruled.

But her mother had made it very clear that she
disliked Roderick Maigrin not so much because of his
breeding but because of his behaviour.

"That man is coarse and vulgar," Grania remembered
her saying to her father, "and I will not have him here
in my house."

"He is a neighbour," the Earl had replied light-
heartedly, "and we have not so many that we can be
choosey."

"I intend to be what you call 'choosey' when it comes
to friendship," the Countess had replied. "We have
plenty of other friends when we have time to see them,
none of whom wish to be associated with Roderick
Maigrin."

Her father had argued, but her mother had been
adamant.

"I do not like him, and I do not trust him," she had
said finally, "and what is more, whatever you may say, I
believe the stories of the way he ill treats his slaves, so I
will not have him here."

Her mother had her way to the extent that Roderick
Maigrin did not come to Secret Harbour, but Grania
knew that her father visited him and they met to drink
together in other parts of the island.

Now her mother was dead and her father had agreed
that she should marry a man who was everything she
hated and despised and from whom she shrank in
terror.

"What am I to do?"

The question was beating again and again in her
head, and when she went into her bedroom and locked

her door, she felt as if the very air coming from the open window repeated and repeated it.

She did not light the candles that were waiting for her on her dressing-table but instead went to look out at a sky encrusted with thousands of stars.

The moonlight was shining on the palm trees as they moved in the wind which still blew faintly from the sea.

It had dropped with the coming of night, but there was always a fresh breeze blowing over the island to take the edge off the heavy, damp heat, which at the height of the sun could be almost intolerable.

As she stood there, Grania felt that she could smell the stringent fragrance of nutmeg, the sharpness of cinnamon, and the clinging scent of cloves.

Perhaps she was imagining them, but they were so much a part of her memories of Grenada that she felt the spices of the island were calling to her and in their own way welcoming her home.

But home to what?

To Roderick Maigrin and the terror which she felt she must die rather than endure!

How long she stood at the window she had no idea.

She only knew that for the moment, the years in which she had been in England seemed to vanish as if they had never happened, and instead she was part of the island as she had been for so many years of her life.

It was not only the magic of the tropical jungle, the giant tree ferns, the liana vines, and the cocoa plantations, but it was also the story of her own life.

A world of Caribs, of buccaneers and pirates, of hurricanes and volcanic eruptions, of battles on land and sea between the French and the English.

It was all so familiar that it had become part of herself and indivisible from her, and the education she had received in London seemed to peel away in the warmth of the air.

She was no longer Lady Grania O'Kerry but instead was one with the spirits of Grenada, one with the flowers, the spices, the palm trees, and the softly

lapping waves of the sea which she could hear far away
in the distance.

"Help me! Help me!" Grania cried aloud.

She was calling to the island as if it could feel for her
in her troubles and help her.

* * *

A long time later, Grania slowly undressed and got
into bed.

There had been no sound in the house while she was
looking out into the night, and she thought that if her
father had come unsteadily up to bed she would have
heard his footsteps on the stairs.

But she did not worry about him as she had done so
often since he had come back into her life.

Instead she could think only of herself, and even as
her eyes closed in sleep she was praying for help with
an intensity that involved her whole body and soul.

* * *

Grania awoke startled by a noise that she sensed
rather than heard.

Then as she came back to consciousness and listened,
she heard it again and for a moment thought that
somebody was at her bedroom door, and was afraid of
who it might be.

Then she realised that the sound had come from
outside, and again there was a low whistle followed by
the sound of someone calling her name.

Still only half-awake, Grania got out of bed and went
to the window which she had left open and uncurtained.

She looked out and there below her she saw Abe.

He was her father's servant. He had come with him
to England and she had known him all her life.

It was Abe who had managed their house for her
mother, found the servants they could afford, and trained
them besides keeping them in order.

It was Abe who had first taken her out in a boat when
she came to the island, and she had helped him bring
back the lobsters which they caught in their own bay

and search for the oysters which her father preferred to any other sea-food.

It was Abe who had taken her riding on a small pony when she was too small to walk round the plantation to watch the slaves working amongst the bananas, the nutmegs, and the cocoa beans.

It was Abe who would go with her to St. George's when she wanted to buy something in the shops or merely to watch the big ships come in to unload their cargo and pick up passengers travelling to other islands.

"I do not know what we should do without Abe," her mother had said almost every day of her childhood.

When they had left for London without him, Grania had often felt that her mother missed Abe as much as she did.

"We ought to have brought him with us," she had said once, but her mother had shaken her head.

"Abe belongs to Grenada and is part of the island," she had said. "What is more, your father could not manage without him."

When she had sent for her father and he had arrived in England too late to say good-bye to her mother before she died, Abe had come with him.

Grania had been so pleased to see Abe that she had almost flung her arms round his neck and kissed him.

She had stopped herself at the last moment only because she realised how much it would embarrass Abe. But the sight of his smiling, coffee-coloured face had made Grania feel home-sick for Grenada in a way she had not felt all the time she had been in London.

Leaning out the window now, Grania asked:

"What is it, Abe?"

"I mus' talk with you, Lady."

He now called her "Lady," although when she was a child he had said "Little Lady," and there was something in the way he spoke which told Grania that it was important.

"I will come down," she said, then hesitated.

Abe knew what she was thinking.

"Quite safe, Lady," he said. "Master not hear."

Grania knew without further explanation why the Earl would not hear, and without saying any more she put on a dressing-gown which was lying unpacked on top of her trunk and a pair of soft slippers.

Then cautiously, making as little noise as possible, she unlocked her bedroom door.

Whatever Abe might say, she was afraid not of seeing her father but of seeing their host.

The candles on the stairs were still alight but guttering low as she came down, and when she reached the Hall she entered the room which she knew looked out onto the garden below her bedroom.

She went to the window which opened onto the verandah, and as she lifted the catch Abe came up the wooden steps to join her.

"We leave quickly, Lady."

"Leave? What do you mean?"

"Danger—big danger!"

"What has happened? What are you trying to tell me?" Grania asked.

Before he answered Abe looked over his shoulder, almost as if he was afraid somebody might be listening. Then he said:

"Rebellion start in Grenville 'mong French slaves."

"A rebellion!" Grania exclaimed.

"Very bad. Kill many English!"

"How do you know this?" Grania asked.

"Some run 'way. Reach here afore dark."

Abe looked over his shoulder again before he said:

"Slaves here think they join rebellion."

Grania did not question that he was telling the truth.

There were always rumours of trouble on the islands which were constantly changing hands, of rebellions amongst the communities which favoured the French, or favoured the English, which were not in power.

The only thing which was surprising was that it should happen on Grenada, which had been English for twelve years after a comparatively short period when it had been in the hands of the French.

But when she had been sailing in the ship from England, the Officers had talked incessantly of the French Revolution and the execution two years ago of Louis XVI.

"It is obvious now that the French slaves on the islands are likely to become restless," the Captain had said, "and ready to start their own revolutions."

Now it had happened in Grenada and Grania was frightened.

"Where shall we go?" she asked.

"Home, Mistress. Much safest place. Few people find Secret Harbour."

Grania knew that was true. Secret Harbour was rightly named.

The house, which had been built many years before her father had restored it, was in an obscure part of the island and was likely to be a safe hiding-place from the French or anybody else.

"We must go at once!" she said. "Have you told Papa?"

Abe shook his head.

"No wake Master," he answered. "You come now, Lady; Master follow."

For a moment Grania hesitated at the idea of leaving her father. Then she thought that she would also be leaving Roderick Maigrin, and that was certainly something she wished to do.

"All right, Abe," she said. "We must go if there is any danger, and I am sure Papa will follow us tomorrow."

"I three horses ready," Abe said. "One carry luggage."

Grania was just about to say her luggage was of no importance, then changed her mind.

After all, she had not been home for three years and she had nothing to wear except the clothes she had brought with her from London.

As if he sensed her hesitation, Abe said:

"Leave to me, Lady, I fetch trunk."

Then, as if he was suddenly frightened, he added:

"Hurry! Go quick! No time lose!"

Grania gave a little gasp, then holding up her dressing-gown with both hands she ran back through the room and up the stairs to her bedroom.

It took her only a few minutes to put on her riding-skirt and to pack the gown she had worn at dinner with her night-things on the top of her trunk which had not yet been unpacked.

Just one piece of her luggage had been brought upstairs and the rest had been left below.

She was just buttoning her muslin blouse when Abe knocked very softly on the door.

"I am ready, Abe," she whispered.

He came in, shut her trunk, strapped it, and picked it up.

He set it on his shoulder and without speaking moved silently down the stairs.

Grania followed him, but as she reached the Hall she knew she could not leave without telling her father where she was going.

She had already seen that there was a desk in the room in which Roderick Maigrin had received them before dinner. Carrying a candle, she searched for a piece of writing-paper.

She found it and also a quill pen which she dipped into the ink-well, and wrote:

> *I have gone home,*
> *Grania.*

Carrying the candle, she went back into the Hall.

For a moment she wondered if she should leave the note on a side-table where her father would see it.

Then she was afraid that it might be removed before he should do so.

Nervously, conscious that her heart was beating violently, she slowly turned the handle of the Dining-Room door.

It opened a crack and she peeped inside.

She could see the table, and the light of the candles

revealed the two men slumped forward, unconscious,
their heads amongst the bottles and glasses.

For a moment Grania just looked at her father and
the man he intended her to marry.

As if she could not bear to go any nearer, she slipped
the piece of paper on which she had written the message just inside the door before she closed it again.

Then she was running as quickly as she could, pursued
by a terror she could not suppress, to where Abe was
waiting for her outside.

Chapter Two

Grania rode without speaking, followed by Abe leading a horse with two of her trunks roped across the saddle, while another horse carried a third trunk and a wicker basket.

She was aware as Abe pointed the way that he had no wish to travel on the road—little more than a track—which lay to the north of Maigrin House and was the nearest way not only to Secret Harbour but to St. George's and the other westward parts of the island.

She wondered at his desire for concealment and thought that perhaps he was afraid they would meet a band of slaves rebelling against their owner or wishing to join those who were already rioting in Grenville.

Abe had said "many English killed," and she knew that once the slaves started looting, killing, and pillaging, it would be hard to stop them.

She was afraid, but not so afraid as she was of Roderick Maigrin and the future her father had determined for her.

She had the feeling as she rode through the thick vegetation that she was escaping from him and he would never be able to catch up with her again.

She knew this idea had no foundation in fact, but at least she was moving away from him, which was a consolation in itself.

There was a path of a sort which kept parallel with

the sea, twisting and turning to follow the numerous
bays and rugged outline of the coast.

Grania was aware that by this route it would take
very much longer to reach home. At the same time, she
was in no hurry.

The scene round her had a strange, ethereal magic
which was a part of her heart.

The shafts of moonlight seemed almost like a revela-
tion coming down to them from the Heavens, making a
pattern of silver on the path ahead and on the great
leaves of the tropical ferns.

They passed cascades that were like molten silver,
then had glimpses of the sea with the moon shimmering
on the slight movement of the water and breaking like
crystal on the sands.

It was a world Grania knew and loved. For the
moment she wanted to forget the past and the future,
and to think only that she was home and that the spirits
that inhabited the tropical forests were protecting and
guiding her.

After they had travelled for nearly an hour the path
entered an open space and Abe walked beside her.

"Who was looking after everything at home while you
were in England?" Grania asked.

There was a little pause before he replied:

"Joseph in charge."

Grania thought for a moment, then she remembered
a tall young man who she thought was some relation of
Abe's.

"Are you sure Joseph is capable of looking after the
house and the plantations?" she asked.

Abe did not answer and she said insistently:

"Tell me what has been happening, Abe. You are
keeping something from me."

"Master not live Secret Harbour for two year!" Abe
said at length.

Grania was astonished.

"Not live at Secret Harbour?" she enquired. "Then
where . . . ?"

She stopped. There was no need for Abe to answer that question.

She knew quite well where her father had been living, and why they had gone to Roderick Maigrin's house rather than to their home.

"Master lonely after Mistress leave," Abe said, as if he felt he must make excuses for the Master he served.

"I can understand that," Grania said almost beneath her breath, "but why did he have to stay with that man?"

"Mr. Maigrin come see Master all time," Abe said. "Then Master say: 'I go where there's somebody to talk to,' and he leave."

"And you did not go with him?" Grania enquired.

"I look after plantations an' house, Lady," Abe replied, "'til last year Master send for me."

"Do you mean to tell me," Grania asked, "that there has been nobody looking after the place for over a year?"

"Go back when possible," Abe replied, "but Master need me."

Grania sighed.

She could understand how her father found Abe indispensable, even as her mother had done, but she could hardly believe that he would leave the house locked up and the plantations to run themselves while he was drinking with Roderick Maigrin.

However, there was no point in saying so. She only thought it was what her mother might have expected would happen if they left her father alone with nobody congenial to keep him company.

"We should never have gone away," she told herself.

At the same time, she knew that it was only because her mother had taken her to London that she had been educated in a way which would have been impossible if she had stayed on the island, and she would always be grateful for the experience.

She had learnt so many things in London, and not only from books.

At the same time, she had the uncomfortable feeling

that her father had paid for that experience not in money but first by loneliness, then by being obliged to seek the company of a man who was a thoroughly bad influence in his life.

But it was too late now for regrets, and as soon as her father joined her they must make up their minds what to do about the rebellion, if it was as serious as Abe seemed to think it was.

When the islands changed hands, which they had done regularly during recent years, there were always planters who lost their land and their money, even if they kept their lives.

But after the first elation and excitement the slaves invariably found that they had only changed one hard task-master for another.

'Perhaps it is nothing very serious,' Grania thought, trying to convince herself.

To change the subject she said to Abe:

"We were lucky when we were coming here that we did not encounter any French ships or indeed any pirates. I hear Will Wilken took Mr. Maigrin's pigs and turkeys and killed a man while he was doing so."

"Pirate bad man!" Abe said. "But he not fight big ships."

"That is true," Grania agreed, "but the sailors on our ship said that pirates like Wilken attack cargo boats, and that is distressing for those who need the food and those who lose money they would otherwise have obtained for their goods."

"Bad man! Cruel!" Abe murmured.

"Will Wilken is English, and I hear there is also a Frenchman, but I do not believe he was about before I left for England."

"No, not here then," Abe said.

He spoke as if he did not wish to say any more, and Grania turned her head to look at him before she said:

"I think the Frenchman is called Beaufort. Have you heard anything about him?"

Again there was a pause before Abe said:

"We take path left, Lady ride ahead."

Grania obeyed and wondered vaguely why he did not seem to wish to talk about the French pirate.

When she was a child, pirates had always seemed to her to be exciting people, despite the fact that the slaves shivered when their names were mentioned, and those who were Catholic crossed themselves.

Her father used to joke about them, saying they usually were not as bad as they were painted.

"They only have small ships, so they dare not attack larger vessels," he had said, "and they are nothing more than sneak-thieves, taking a pig here, a turkey there, and seldom doing more harm than the gypsies or tinkers would do when I was a boy in Ireland."

They rode on and now at last the way became familiar and Grania recognised clumps of palm trees and the brilliance of the poinsettias which on the island grew to over forty feet.

Now the moonlight was fading and the stars seemed to recede into the darkness of the sky.

Soon it would be dawn, and already she could feel a breeze coming from the sea to sweep away the heaviness of the air enclosed by the tropical plants which grew sometimes like green cliffs on each side of the path.

Then at last the jungle was left behind as they reached her father's plantations.

Even in the dimness of the fading moonlight she had the idea that they looked neglected. Then she told herself she was being unnecessarily critical.

Now she could smell the nutmeg, the cinnamon, and the chives, while mixed with their scent was the fragrance of thyme, which she remembered was always sold in bunches with the chives.

As they moved on she thought she recognised the strong fragrance of the tonka bean, which her father grew because it was easier than some of the other crops.

"The island spices," she said to herself with a smile, and was sure she could distinguish allspice or pimento, which Abe had pointed out to her when she was very small, their smell combining the fragrances of cinnamon, nutmeg, and cloves all mixed together.

Now the dawn was breaking and as the sky became translucent Grania could see in the distance the roofs of her home.

"There it is, Abe!" she exclaimed with sudden excitement in her voice.

"Yes, Lady. But you not disappointed if dusty. I get women soon clean everything."

"Yes, of course," Grania agreed.

At the same time, she was sure now that her father had never intended to take her home.

He had meant them to stay with Roderick Maigrin, and if there had not been a revolution she would doubtless have been married very quickly, whatever she might have said, however much she might have protested.

"I cannot marry him!" she said beneath her breath.

She thought that if her father came home alone she could explain why it was impossible for her to tolerate such a man and try to make him understand.

It would be easier, she thought, if she could talk to him without that horrible, red-faced Roderick Maigrin listening and plying her father with drinks.

She sent up a little prayer to her mother for help and felt that she would somehow save her, although how she could do so Grania had no idea.

As they drew nearer to the house, it was easy to see that the windows were covered by wooden shutters, and the shrubs had encroached nearer than they would have been allowed to do in the past.

It flashed through Grania's mind that it was like the Palace of the Sleeping Beauty.

Bougainvillaea covered the steps of the verandah and had wound its way up onto the roof of it, while the pale yellow blossoms of the acacia and a vine which was called "Cup of Gold" had crept prolifically over everything within sight.

It was beautiful but had something unreal about it,

and for a moment Grania felt as if it were only a dream that might vanish and she would wake to find it was no longer there.

Then she forced herself to say in what she hoped was a matter-of-fact tone:

"Put the horses in the stable, Abe, and give me the key to the house, if you have it."

"Have key back door, Lady."

"Then I will go in at the back," Grania smiled, "and start opening the shutters. I expect everything will smell musty after being shut up for so long."

She thought too, without saying so, that there would be lizards running up the walls, and if there had been a crack anywhere in the roof, birds would have nested in the corners of the rooms.

She only hoped they had not damaged the things her mother had prized—the furniture she had brought from England when she was first married.

There were other treasures which she had accumulated over the years, buying them sometimes from planters who were going home or receiving them as presents from their friends in St. George's and other parts of the island.

The stables at the back of the house were almost covered with purple bougainvillaea so that Abe had to pull it aside to find the entrance to the stalls.

Grania dismounted, leaving Abe to unsaddle the horse she had ridden and lift the trunks from the other two horses.

She suspected that in a short while the slaves would be awake and there would be somebody to assist him, but for the moment she was interested only in going into the house.

She went up the steps to the back door, seeing that they badly needed repairing, and the door itself looked dilapidated with the paint peeling from the heat.

The key turned easily and she pushed open the door and walked inside.

As she had expected, the house smelt musty, but not as badly as it might have done.

She walked in through the back premises past the large kitchen which her mother had always insisted be kept spotlessly clean, then into the Hall.

The house was not as dusty as she had expected, although it was hard to see in the dim light.

She opened the door into what had been the Drawing-Room.

To her surprise, the sofas were not protected as they should have been by Holland covers, the curtains were drawn back from the windows, and the shutters were not closed.

She thought it was careless of Abe not to have taken more trouble over this particular room.

But it certainly did not seem to have come to very much harm, although it was difficult to see every detail.

Grania instinctively tidied a cushion that was crooked on a chair, then told herself that before she started opening up the house she had better change.

The day was already beginning to grow warmer, and her riding-skirt, which was not of a very thin material, would soon become uncomfortably heavy, while the muslin blouse she was wearing had long sleeves.

She thought she would have grown out of all the clothes she had left behind but there would doubtless be something of her mother's she could wear.

When they had left for London, the Countess had not packed her light cotton gowns, knowing that she would have no use for them there and they would also be out of fashion.

"I will put on one of Mama's gowns," Grania told herself. "Then I will start to make the house look as it used to be before we left."

She went to the Drawing-Room and up the stairs.

A rather beautiful staircase swept round artistically and up to a landing on which the centre room had been specially designed for her mother.

As she neared it Grania was thinking of how as a child she had always run eagerly to this room first thing in the morning, as soon as she was dressed by the coloured maid who looked after her.

Her mother would be in bed, propped against the pillows that were edged with lace and had insertions through which she would thread pretty coloured ribbons to match her nightgowns.

"You look so pretty in bed, Mama, you might be going to a Ball," Grania had said once.

"I want to look pretty for your father," her mother had replied. "He is a very handsome man, dearest, and he likes a woman to be pretty and always to make the best of herself. You must remember that."

Grania had remembered, and she knew that her father was proud of her too when he took her to St. George's and his friends paid her compliments and said that when she grew up she would be the Belle of the island.

Grania in her own mind had always connected her father with things that were beautiful, and she asked herself now how he could possibly contemplate marrying her off to a man who was ugly not only in appearance but also in character.

She opened the door of the bedroom and was once again surprised to find the shutters drawn from the large windows that covered one wall of the room.

Through them she could see the palm trees against a sky that now held a tinge of gold in it.

There was a fragrance in the room that she had always connected with her mother, and she knew that it was the scent of jasmine whose small star-shaped white flowers bloomed all the year round.

Her mother had distilled the perfume which she always used, and which in consequence now brought her back so vividly to Grania's mind that instinctively she looked towards the bed as if she expected to see her there.

Then suddenly she was very still, as if rooted to the spot, staring as if her eyes must be deceiving her.

It was not her mother she could see against the white pillows, but a man.

For a moment she thought she must be imagining him. Then almost as if the light grew clearer she saw quite distinctly and unmistakably a man's head on her mother's pillows.

She stood for a moment staring, wondering whether she should go or stay.

Then as if in his sleep her presence communicated itself to him, the man stirred and opened his eyes, and now they were looking at each other across the room.

He was good-looking—"handsome" she supposed was the right word.

He had dark hair sweeping back from a square forehead, a clean-shaven face with distinctive features, and dark eyes which for a moment stared at her blankly.

Then his expression changed, and there was a smile on his lips and a sudden twinkle of recognition in his eyes.

"Who are you? What are you doing here?" Grania asked.

"Your pardon, *Mademoiselle*," the man replied, sitting up against the pillows, "but I have no reason to ask who you are when your picture hangs before me on the wall."

Without really meaning to, Grania turned her head to where facing the bed over the top of the chest-of-drawers there was a picture of her mother painted when she had first been engaged to her father, before she had come to Grenada.

"That is a picture of my mother," she said. "What are you doing here in her bed?"

Even as she spoke she realised that the way the man had spoken to her showed that he was not English.

She gave a little gasp.

"You are French!" she exclaimed.

"Yes, *Mademoiselle*, I am French," the man replied, "and I can only apologise for occupying your mother's room, but the house was empty."

"I know that," Grania replied, "but you had no . . . right. It is an . . . intrusion for you to . . . come here. And I do not understand . . ."

Then again she stopped and drew in her breath before she said:

"I think . . . perhaps I have . . . heard of you."

The man made a little gesture with his hand.

"I promise you I am not famous but infamous," he said. "Beaufort—at your service!"

"The pirate!"

"The same, *Mademoiselle*! And a very contrite pirate, if my presence here upsets you."

"Of course you upset me!" Grania said sharply. "As I have said, you had no right to intrude because we were away from home."

"I knew the house was empty, and may I add that nobody expected that you would come here when you returned home to Grenada."

There was silence. Then Grania said hesitatingly:

"You . . . speak as if you knew I was . . . coming back to the island."

The pirate smiled at her and it not only seemed to make him look younger but gave a touch of mischievousness to his expression.

"I should think everybody on the island knows it. Gossip is carried on the wind and in the songs of the birds."

"Then you knew my father had gone to England."

The pirate nodded.

"I knew that, and that you sent for him because your mother was ill. I am hoping that she is better."

"She is . . . dead!"

"My deepest condolences, *Mademoiselle*."

He spoke with a sincerity which did not make it seem as if he was being intrusive.

Suddenly Grania was aware that she was talking to a pirate and he was lying in her mother's bed, his shoulders above the sheets showing that he was naked.

She had half-turned towards the door when the pirate said:

"If you will permit me to dress myself, *Mademoiselle*, I will come downstairs to explain my presence, and make my apologies before I leave."

"Thank you," Grania said, and went from the room, closing the door behind her.

Outside on the landing, she stood for a moment thinking that now in fact she *must* be dreaming and this could not really be happening.

How could she have come home to find a pirate in the house, and a Frenchman at that?

She supposed she should have been frightened not only because the man was a pirate but also because he was French.

Yet, in some way which she could not explain, he did not frighten her.

She had the feeling that if she asked him to leave he would do so at once, only making sure before he left that she accepted his apologies for having used the house in her absence.

"It is an intolerable thing to have done!" she told herself, but she was not angry.

She went to her own room and found it as she had expected the whole house to be after what Abe had said.

When she opened the shutters she saw that the dust was thick on the floor, on the dressing-table, and on the cover which protected the bed.

Two little lizards shot behind the curtains when she appeared, and there was a smell of mustiness which was overpowering until she opened the window.

She pulled open the wardrobe and knew she could not change into any of the cotton gowns that hung there because she had grown so much taller in the last three years, and although she was still very slim, her figure was no longer that of a child but had the first curves of maturity.

"I must stay as I am," Grania decided, and tried to feel angry because the presence of the pirate was inconvenient to her, but in fact she only felt curious.

There was nothing she could do in her bedroom and she therefore went downstairs.

As she reached the Hall she heard the sound of voices in the kitchen and felt she should warn Abe that there was a pirate in the house.

Then as she went towards the kitchen-quarters she heard a man's voice saying in broken English:

"We not expect you. I go wake *Monsieur.*"

"Good idea," Abe replied, "afore my Lady see him."

Grania walked into the kitchen.

Standing beside Abe was a white man who she thought looked extremely French.

He was small and dark-haired, and she thought that if she had seen him anywhere in the world she would have known that he was of French origin.

He looked startled at her appearance and she thought also a little fearful.

"I have already talked to your Master," she said. "He is dressing and coming downstairs to make his apologies before he leaves."

The little Frenchman looked relieved and moved towards the kitchen-table, where Grania saw a large tin and beside it a tray on which was a coffee-pot.

She guessed that the Frenchman's servant had been preparing his breakfast for him, and with a faint smile she said:

"It would only be hospitable to allow your Master to have his coffee before he leaves. Where does he usually drink it?"

"On the verandah, *M'mselle.*"

"Very well. Take it there. And, Abe, I too would like a cup of coffee."

She knew both men stared at her with surprise, then smiling she walked towards the front door.

As she might have expected, it was not bolted, and she guessed that it was the entrance through which the Frenchman came into the house.

She went out onto the verandah and now in the distance over the palm trees she could just see the tops of two masts.

The trees were so high that unless she had been looking for them they would have been invisible, and she knew that Secret Harbour was the perfect place for a pirate ship to hide and wondered why she had never thought of it before.

The small bay had been given its name, which described it very aptly, by its former owner.

The entrance to it was at the side, and a long tongue of land covered with pine trees faced the sea.

Once the ship was in the harbour it was almost impossible to see it either from the land side or from the sea.

Unless one was actually aware of its existence, one could pass a dozen times without being aware that there was a ship at anchor in the bay.

'I would like to see the ship,' Grania thought, then chided herself for her curiosity.

She knew she should be feeling shocked, angry, and perhaps insulted that a pirate should use her home, and yet she felt none of these emotions, which much surprised her.

When a few minutes later the Pirate joined her on the verandah, she thought that he would have been more at home in the Drawing-Rooms and Ball-Rooms of London.

He was somehow too elegant and certainly too smart for the verandah with its overgrown vines and the dirty, neglected windows behind them.

There was a table made of native wicker-work and two chairs, and before the Frenchman could speak, the servants, Abe and his own man, appeared carrying a white table-cloth with which they covered the table, then placed on it a silver tray containing two cups and saucers.

They were the ones her mother had kept for best, Grania noticed, and now there was the aroma of coffee and the servants set down a pot and beside it a plate of croissants warm from the oven, a pat of butter, and a glass dish filled with honey.

"*Petit déjeuner est servi, Monsieur,*" the Frenchman's servant announced, and then he and Abe vanished.

Grania looked at the pirate. He seemed about to speak, then suddenly she laughed.

"I do not believe this is happening," she said. "You cannot really be a pirate."

"I assure you that I am."

"But I always imagined they were evil, dirty, greasy

men who used rough oaths; men from whom women hid in terror."

"You are thinking of one of your own countrymen—Will Wilken."

"We are lucky he did not discover Secret Harbour," Grania said. "I heard last night that he was pillaging farther down the coast."

"I have heard many things about him," the Frenchman replied. "But may I suggest that the coffee is waiting?"

"Yes, of course."

She sat down by instinct in front of the coffee-pot, and as he seated himself opposite her she asked:

"Shall I pour out your coffee or would you prefer to do it for yourself?"

"I should be honoured for you to act as my hostess."

She tried to smile at him, but there was something about him that made her feel a little shy.

So instead she busied herself by filling his cup and passing it to him.

"You must have brought your croissants with you," she said.

"My servant brought them," the Frenchman replied. "They are baked fresh every day."

Grania gave a little laugh.

"So even a pirate, if he is French, worries about his food!"

"But of course," the Pirate replied. "Food is an art, and the worst hardship of being perpetually at sea is eating what I have to instead of procuring what I like to eat."

Grania laughed again. Then she asked:

"Why are you a pirate? It seems . . . or perhaps I am being impertinent . . . a strange occupation for you."

"It is a long story," the Frenchman replied. "But may I first ask why you are here, and where is your father?"

"I am here," Grania explained, "because a revolution has broken out in Grenville."

The Frenchman was suddenly tense, staring at her across the table.

"A revolution?"

"Yes. It started several nights ago, but we arrived only yesterday evening at Mr. Maigrin's house. Then in the middle of the night Abe learnt that the revolutionaries had taken over Grenville and killed a number of Englishmen."

"It cannot be possible!" the Frenchman said as if he spoke to himself. "But if there is a revolution it will have been started by Julius Fédor."

"How do you know that?"

"I heard that he was preaching sedition amongst the French slaves."

"So you think the revolution is serious?"

"I am afraid it will be," the Pirate replied.

"But surely you want the French to be the victors and take over this island again as they did twelve years ago?"

He shook his head.

"If the French take it over, it will be with ships and soldiers, not by a rebellion amongst the slaves. They may be successful for a short while, but English soldiers will eventually arrive to attack them and there will be a great deal of blood-shed."

Grania sighed.

It all seemed so unnecessary and rather frightening.

The Frenchman rose to his feet.

"Will you excuse me for one moment while I speak to my servant? He must find out exactly how much danger there may be for you."

He walked away into the house and she stared after him.

She could not help contrasting the lithe grace with which he moved with the uncouth unsteadiness of Roderick Maigrin.

His hair, which was dark and thick, was pulled back into a neat bow set in the nape of his neck, and his cravat was crisp and fresh, the points of his collar high over his chin in the same manner as the Beaux of St. James's wore theirs.

His coat fitted without a wrinkle, his white cloth breeches revealed his slim attractive hips, and his white stockings and buckled shoes were very smart.

"He is a gentleman!" Grania told herself. "It is ridiculous to call him a pirate . . . an outlaw of the seas!"

The Frenchman came back.

"My man and yours are sending people to find out exactly what is known of this revolution. But Abe assures me that the information he received last night and early this morning is absolutely reliable, and there is no doubt that the rebels are killing the English in Grenville, where a hundred slaves took everybody in the town by surprise."

Grania gave a little murmur and he went on:

"As usual, they have plundered store-houses, dragged the frightened inhabitants into the street, and set them up as marks to be shot at."

"Oh . . . no!" Grania exclaimed.

"Some escaped by swimming to the vessels that were tied up in the harbour. Others made their way south, and there were some who got as far as Maigrin House."

"Do you think . . . all the slaves on the . . . island will rise and join . . . them?" Grania asked in a low voice.

"We must wait and see," the Frenchman replied. "If the worst comes to the worst, *Mademoiselle*, my ship is at your disposal."

"Do you think that will be a safe place to hide?"

The Frenchman smiled.

"It may be a case of 'any port in a storm.'"

"Yes, of course, but I am hoping that my father will join me today, and perhaps he will have other ideas of where we should go."

"Naturally," the Frenchman agreed, "and I should imagine that both you and your father, and doubtless also Mr. Maigrin, will be welcome in the Fort of St. George's."

Grania could not disguise the expression in her eyes as he spoke of Roderick Maigrin.

Instead of answering, she ate the delicious croissant which she had spread with butter and honey.

There was silence. Then the Frenchman said:

"I have been told, although of course it may be incorrect, that you are to marry Mr. Maigrin."

"Who told you that?"

The Frenchman shrugged his shoulders.

"I learnt that it was intended before your father went to England to bring you home."

It flashed through Grania's mind that even if her mother had lived, her father might have insisted on his rights as her legal Guardian and brought her back to Grenada.

Then as she thought of Roderick Maigrin, the revulsion that she had felt for him last night swept over her again.

Quite involuntarily and without really thinking what she was saying, she asked:

"What can I . . . do? How can I . . . escape? I cannot . . . marry that . . . man!"

The terror in her voice seemed to vibrate on the air, and she was aware that the Frenchman was staring at her intently, his dark eyes searching her face.

Then he said:

"I agree it is impossible for somebody like you to marry such a man, but it is not for me to tell you how you can avoid doing so."

"Then . . . who else can I . . . ask?" Grania said almost like a child. "I did not know until the very moment we arrived that that was what Papa . . . intended, and now that I am . . . here, I do not know . . . what I can do . . . or where I can . . . hide from . . . him."

The Frenchman put his knife down on the table with a little clatter.

"That is your problem, *Mademoiselle*," he said, "and as you must be aware, I cannot interfere."

"No . . . of course not," Grania agreed. "I should not have . . . spoken as I . . . did. Forgive . . . me."

"There is nothing to forgive. I want to listen. I want to help you, but I am an enemy, apart from the fact that I am also a criminal outlaw."

"Perhaps that is what I . . . should be," Grania said,

"then even Mr. Maigrin would not . . . wish to marry . . . me."

Even as she spoke she knew that there was nothing she could do to prevent him from wanting her for herself apart from her social position.

She saw again the look in his eyes last night and felt herself shiver.

She was frightened, desperately, horribly frightened, not of the revolution, not of dying, but of being touched by a man who she knew was evil and whose very presence disgusted her so that she felt physically sick when he was near her.

Her face must have been very expressive, for suddenly the Frenchman asked harshly:

"Why did you not stay in England where you were safe?"

"How could I after Mama died?" Grania asked. "I knew very few people, and besides . . . Papa would have . . . insisted on bringing me back . . . whatever I . . . might have . . . said."

"It is a pity you could not have found somebody to marry you while you were there," the Frenchman remarked.

"I think that is what Mama wanted," Grania answered. "She intended to present me to the King and Queen and then I would have been asked to Balls and parties. She had planned so many things, but she became ill . . . so terribly ill . . . before Christmas."

She paused for a moment before she went on:

"The weather was foggy and cold, and Mama had been living in the sun for so many years that the Doctor said her blood had become thin and she was too . . . weak to stand the English . . . climate."

"I understand," the Frenchman said in a low voice. "But surely you could tell your father that you have no wish to marry this man?"

"I have told him," Grania replied, "but he said he had it all arranged . . . and that Mr. Maigrin was . . . very rich."

As she spoke she felt that she was being disloyal, but

it was, she knew, the whole crux of the matter, the real
reason why her father was so insistent that she must
marry.

Roderick Maigrin was rich and could keep her father
in the comfort he wanted, and the only way her father
could achieve this was by handing over his daughter.

"It is an intolerable situation!" the Frenchman said
suddenly in a voice that made her start.

"But . . . what can I do about it?" Grania asked.

"When I lay in bed and looked at your mother's
picture," he said in a low voice, "I thought it would be
impossible for anybody to be lovelier, sweeter, or more
attractive. But now that I have seen you I know that
while outwardly you resemble your mother, there is,
perhaps because you are alive, something which the
artist failed to portray."

"What is it?" Grania asked curiously.

"I think the right word for it is that you have a
spiritualité, *Mademoiselle*, which would be impossible to convey on canvass, except for a Michelangelo or
a Botticelli."

"Thank you," Grania said in a low voice.

"I am not just paying you a compliment," the
Frenchman said, "but stating a fact, and that is why I
know it would be impossible for you to marry a man
like Maigrin. I have seen him only once, but I have
heard a great deal about him, and I can say in all truth:
better dead than that you should be his wife!"

Grania clasped her hands together.

"That is what I feel . . . but I know Papa will not . . . listen
to me . . . and when he comes here I shall be forced to
marry, whatever I may say . . . however much I may . . .
plead with . . . him."

The Frenchman rose to his feet and walked to the rail
of the verandah to stand leaning against it.

Grània thought he was looking at his ship and thinking how easily he could slip out of the harbour and into
the open sea, where he would be free and could leave
behind him the troubles and difficulties of the island
and her personal worries.

He looked very elegant standing there, his head silhouetted against the bougainvillaea.

But she had the feeling that instead of a ship there should be a Phaeton waiting for him, drawn by two Thoroughbred horses, and that he would invite her to accompany him and they would drive in Hyde Park, bowing to their friends.

Then there would be only the gossip and laughter of social London and no talk of revolutions and blood-shed or of marriage to Roderick Maigrin.

She was thinking at that moment, although of course it seemed absurd, that the Frenchman stood for security in a world that for her had suddenly become horrifying and frightening and in which she was completely helpless.

"What time do you expect your father?" the Frenchman asked at length.

She thought his voice had an edge to it, and it was a little louder than she had expected.

"I . . . I have no idea," she answered hesitatingly. "When I left in the darkness very early this morning . . . they had . . . been . . . drinking all . . . night and had not . . . gone to bed."

The Frenchman nodded, as if that was what he had expected, and said:

"Then we have time. For the moment I suggest you stop worrying about the future and instead perhaps you would like to visit my ship."

"Can I do that?" Grania asked.

"I should be very honoured if you would do so."

"Then please . . . may I change? It will soon be very hot."

"But of course," he replied.

Grania ran from the verandah and up the stairs.

As she had expected, Abe had already taken up her trunks and put them down in her mother's room.

He had undone the straps and opened them, and she suspected that later he would find one of the women who had served in the house before to come and unpack for her.

For the moment, all she wanted was a dress in which, although she would not admit it to herself, she would look her best.

Quickly she pulled out of the nearest trunk one of the pretty gowns she had bought in London.

She had worn it last year, but its full skirt was still fashionable, and the fichu, although a little creased from the voyage, was crisp and clean.

It took Grania only a few minutes to take off the clothes in which she had travelled and to wash in the basin. She was not surprised to find a ewer filled with cool, clean water.

Then she dressed herself again and ran downstairs to where she was sure the Pirate would be waiting for her.

She was not mistaken.

He was sitting on the verandah, having moved his chair into the sunshine, and she knew now that his skin was so dark, because, unlike the Beaux in London, he had allowed himself to become sunburnt.

It became him, and she thought that in a way the fact that his skin had been burnt by the sun had prevented her from being shocked when she saw him naked in bed.

He rose at her approach and she saw a look of admiration in his eyes and a smile on his lips as he took in her appearance.

It was so different from the way Roderick Maigrin had looked at her last night, when she had felt that with his eyes on her breasts he was seeing her not as she was, but naked.

"Would you like me to tell you that you look very lovely and like the Spirit of Spring?" the Frenchman asked.

"I enjoy hearing you say it," Grania replied.

"But you must have heard so many compliments in London that they cease to be anything but a bore."

"The only compliments I received were for the work I did at School, and one or two from gentlemen who called to take my mother to a Ball or to Vauxhall."

"You were too young to become a Society Beauty?"

"Much too young," Grania replied, "and now, as that is something I have missed completely, I suppose it will never happen to me."

"Does that distress you?"

"It is disappointing. Mama used to describe so often the Balls and parties I should attend that I feel as if they are familiar, and I have often dreamt of them."

"I assure you there are other things to do in the world which are far more entrancing," the Frenchman said.

"Then you must tell me about them," Grania replied, "to make up for what I have missed."

"Perhaps that is something I should not do," he said enigmatically.

Then, when she would have asked him for an explanation, he said:

"Come along. Let us go quickly and see my ship, just in case your father returns before you are able to do so."

As if she was afraid that might happen, she hurried down the steps of the verandah with the Frenchman beside her.

They walked through the untidy garden which had gone completely wild since her mother had left, and soon found themselves amongst the pine trees.

There was just enough wind to move their leaves very gently, and then ahead Grania had her first glimpse of the ship.

She could see the poop-deck, the fo'c'sle, and the high raking masts. The sails were furled, but she had the feeling that they could be set very swiftly.

Then the ship would be gone, and she would be left behind, never to see it again.

Ahead of them was a long narrow jetty which had been built out into the harbour. The ship was anchored at the very end of it, and there was a gang-plank to connect the deck with the jetty.

She and the Frenchman walked over the rough, unplaned wood and when they reached the gang-plank he stopped and asked:

"There are no hand-rails. Are you afraid?"

"No, of course not," Grania replied, smiling.

Then he said:

"Let me go first and I will help you aboard, and of course I will be honoured to do so."

There was something in the way he spoke the last words that made her feel a little shy.

He stretched out his hand and she took it, and as she touched it she felt the vibration of his fingers and it gave her a strange sensation which she had never had before.

The ship was entrancing, almost like a child's toy.

The deck had been scrubbed spotlessly clean, the paint was fresh, and there were men busy with ropes who paid no attention at their approach, but Grania was certain that their eyes were watching her as she walked beside their Captain.

He helped her down some steps and opened a door which she realised led into the stern cabin.

The sun was streaming through large portholes and making vivid patterns on the walls of the cabin.

She had always expected that a pirate-ship would be dirty and disorderly. In the stories she had read, the Captain's cabin had been a dark hole filled with cutlasses and empty bottles.

This cabin was like a room in a house, with comfortable armchairs and in one corner a four-poster bed with drawn curtains.

Everything was exquisitely neat and she thought she smelt bees'-wax and lavender.

There was a carpet on the floor, cushions on the chairs, and on the table there was a vase of flowers which she thought must have been picked from what had been her mother's garden.

She stood looking round her until she realised the Frenchman was watching her with a smile.

"Well?" he questioned.

"It is very attractive and very comfortable."

"It is my home now," he said quietly, "and just as a Frenchman likes his food, he also likes his comforts."

"But you are always in danger," Grania said. "If you are seen by either the English or the French they will try to destroy or capture you, and if you are caught . . . you will die!"

"I am aware of that," he said, "but I find danger exciting, and I can assure you, although it seems a contradiction in terms, that I will not take any risks."

"Then why . . . ?" Grania began, and realised that once again she was being curious and prying into his private affairs.

"Come and sit down," the Frenchman said. "I want to see you at ease in my room, and then when you are no longer here, I can look into my mind and see you here again."

He spoke in quite an ordinary voice, and yet she felt herself blushing at what he had said.

Obediently she sat down in one of the armchairs, the sun coming through the porthole turning her hair to gold.

Because it was so early in the morning she had not brought a hat or a sunshade, and she felt that somehow it was right for her to be sitting in this tiny room talking to a man who was more attractive than any man she had seen in London.

"Why do you call yourself 'Beaufort'?" she enquired when the silence seemed somehow embarrassing.

"Because it is my name," he answered, "the name by which I was Christened, and it does seem an appropriate sobriquet, since I cannot use my other name."

"Why not?"

"Because it would be unseemly. My ancestors would turn in their graves, and also one day I hope to go back to where I belong."

"You cannot go to France," Grania said quickly, remembering the Revolution.

"I am aware of that," he said, "but that is not where I really belong—at least not since I was very young."

"Then where? Or is that a question I should not ask?"

"Shall I say that when we are together like this we can ask any questions of each other?" the Frenchman said. "And because I am honoured that you should be interested, I will tell you that I come from Martinique, where I had a plantation, and my real name is de Vence—Beaufort de Vence."

"It is a very attractive name."

"There have been *Comtes* de Vence in France for centuries," the Frenchman said. "They are part of the history of that country."

"Are you a *Comte?*"

"As my father is dead, I am head of the family."

"But your home is in Martinique."

"It was!"

Grania looked at him, puzzled, then she gave a little cry.

"You are a refugee! The British took Martinique last year!"

"Exactly!" the *Comte* said. "I should undoubtedly have died if I had not escaped just before they seized my plantation."

"So that was why you became a pirate!"

"That is why I became a pirate, and I shall remain a pirate until the British are driven out, which they will be eventually, and I can regain my possessions."

Grania gave a little sigh.

"There is always so much fighting in these islands, and the loss of life is terrible."

"I thought that myself," the *Comte* replied, "but at least for the moment I am as safe here as I am likely to be anywhere."

Grania did not speak.

She was thinking that if he was safe, she, on the contrary, was in the greatest danger—danger from the revolutionaries and, more frightening still, danger from Roderick Maigrin.

Chapter Three

When Grania looked round the cabin she saw, as she thought she might have expected, a great number of books.

The cases had been skilfully inserted into the panelling, and although they did not have a glass front, there was a bar which held them in place so that they would not fall out when the ship rolled at sea.

The *Comte* followed the direction of her eyes and said with a smile:

"I feel you are also a reader."

"I had to learn about the world from books before I went to London," Grania replied, "and then, just when I was going to step into a world I had read about in the School-Room, I had to come back here."

"Perhaps you would have found that world, which is to some women very glittering and glamorous, disappointing."

"Why should you think that?"

"Because I have a feeling, and I do not think I am wrong," the *Comte* replied, "that you are seeking something deeper and more important than can be found on the surface of a social life that relies on tinkling laughter and the clinking of glasses."

Grania looked at him in surprise.

"Perhaps you are right," she said, "but Mama always made it sound so exciting that I looked forward to making my début, and to meeting people who now

46

remain only names to me in the newspapers and the history books."

"Then you will not feel disillusioned by reality."

Grania raised her eye-brows.

"Is that what you have been?"

"Not really," he admitted, "and I am, I suppose, fortunate in that I knew Paris before the Revolution, and I have also been to London."

"And you enjoyed it?"

"When I was young I found it very intriguing, and yet I knew that my real place was here among the islands."

"You love Martinique?"

"It is my home, and will be my home again."

The way he spoke was very moving, and Grania said softly, without thinking:

"I shall pray that it will be returned to you."

A smile seemed to illumine his face before he said:

"Thank you, and I am ready to believe, *Mademoiselle*, that your prayers will always be heard."

"Except those for myself," Grania replied.

Then she thought that perhaps she was being unfair. She had prayed last night to escape from Roderick Maigrin, and for the moment she was away from him.

There was always the chance that if she was alone with her father she might convince him that such a marriage was so intolerable that he would not inflict it on her.

After all, he had loved her when she was a child—there was no doubt about that—and she was sure that it was only because her mother and she had gone away that he had fallen so completely under Mr. Maigrin's thumb and was ready to acquiesce in anything he suggested.

The expressions which followed one another across her face were more revealing than she had realised, and she felt uncomfortably that the *Comte* could read her thoughts when he said:

"You are very lovely, *Mademoiselle*, and I cannot

believe that any man, even your father, would not listen
when you plead with him."

"I shall try . . . I shall try very . . . hard."

He walked to one of the portholes before he said:

"I think you should now return home. If your father
arrives and finds you not there, he will be very shocked
to learn that you are with somebody like myself."

"I am sure if you met Papa in other circumstances you
would like each other."

"But circumstances being what they are, we must
remain at a distance," the *Comte* said firmly.

He walked towards the door of the cabin and there
was nothing Grania could do but rise from the chair in
which she had been sitting.

She had the strange feeling that she was leaving
safety and security for danger, but she could not put
such feelings into words and could only follow the
Comte up the companionway and onto the deck.

The sailors watched her from the corners of their
eyes as she walked towards the gangway.

She was sure that because they were Frenchmen
they were admiring her, and she told herself that it was
impertinent of them to do so because they were outlaws
and pirates who in fact should be frightened in case she
betrayed them.

Again the *Comte* must have read her thoughts, for as
they stepped ashore he said:

"One day I hope I shall have the privilege of introduc-
ing my friends to you, for that is what my crew are:
friends who have no wish to be outlaws but have been
forced to flee from your countrymen."

The way he spoke made Grania feel ashamed.

"I am sorry for . . . anybody who has been a . . . victim
of war," she said, "but those who live on these islands
seem to know . . . nothing else."

"That is true," the *Comte* agreed, "and it is always
the innocent who suffer."

They walked through the thickness of the trees and
the bougainvillaea bushes until the house was in sight.

"I will leave you here," the *Comte* said.

"Please do not . . . go," Grania said impulsively.

He looked at her in surprise and she said:

"We have not yet heard what Abe and your man have found out about the revolutionaries. Suppose they are on their way here? I could only escape if you let me come aboard your ship."

Even as she spoke she knew that she was not so much frightened of the revolutionaries as of losing the *Comte*.

She wanted to stay with him, she wanted to talk to him, and most of all she wanted him to protect her from Roderick Maigrin.

"If the revolutionaries are here," he said, "I doubt if even as a pirate I would be safe."

"You mean they will think of you as an aristocrat?"

"Exactly!" he said. "The reason why Fédor has started a revolution is that he has been in Guadaloupe, which is the centre of the French Revolution in the West Indies."

"Is that true?" Grania asked.

"I am told that Fédor was given a commission as Commander General of the insurgents in Grenada."

"You mean this has been planned for some time?"

The *Comte* nodded.

"They have arms and ammunition, caps of liberty, national cockades, and a flag on which is inscribed: 'Liberté, Egalité, ou la Mort.'"

Grania gave a little cry.

"Do you mean the English do not know this?"

The *Comte* shrugged his shoulders, and she knew without his saying any more that the English in St. George's had become complacent and were too busy enjoying themselves to anticipate that there might be an uprising.

It seemed extraordinary that they should have been taken by surprise, when the *Comte* knew so much.

At the same time, she was well aware that in Grenada they often knew things that happened on other islands before they knew it themselves.

As the *Comte* had said, the very birds carried gossip across the blue sea, and the fact that there were French under British jurisdiction and vice versa was an open invitation for the slaves who planned to rebel if the opportunity arose.

They walked through the part of the garden which had once been cultivated and now was a riot of colour and blossom.

There were little patches of English flowers which her mother had tried to cultivate and which in their very profusion seemed to have become part of the tropical scene.

The house when they reached it seemed very quiet, and Grania knew at once that her father had not arrived.

She walked in through the front door, followed by the *Comte*, and went straight towards the kitchen to find that it was empty.

"Abe and your man have not returned," she said.

"Then I suggest we sit and wait for them," the *Comte* said, "and it will be cooler in the Drawing-Room than anywhere else."

"I wondered when I came here this morning why there were no covers on the furniture," Grania said. "Have you sat there very often?"

"Occasionally," the *Comte* admitted. "It made me think of my home when I was a child, and also of my house in Martinique, which is very beautiful. I would like to show it to you one day."

"I would like that," Grania said simply.

Her eyes met his as she spoke, then shyly she looked away.

"Perhaps I should offer you some of your own coffee?"

"I want nothing," he said, "except to talk to you. Sit down *Mademoiselle*, and tell me about yourself."

Grania laughed.

"There is very little to tell that you do not already know, and I would rather hear about you."

"That would be dull for me," the *Comte* said, "and as the hostess you must be generous to your guest."

"An uninvited guest who has made himself very much at home!"

"That is true, but I had a feeling when I lay in bed looking at your picture that you would be as kind and welcoming as you have been."

"I am sure Mama would have liked you," Grania said impulsively.

"You could not say anything that would please me more," the *Comte* answered. "I have heard about your mother and I know how understanding she was to everybody she met, and I am sure that she was very proud of her daughter."

"She would not be...proud if she...knew what Papa is...planning for me," Grania said in a small voice.

"We have already agreed that you must talk to your father and make him understand what your mother would have felt had she been here," the *Comte* said.

He spoke almost severely, as if he were instructing her like a School-Master and expecting her to obey him.

"My father has changed...since we have been... away," Grania said. "I felt when we were sailing back that he had...something on his...mind."

There was silence for a moment. Then the *Comte* said:

"If he had stayed and attended to his plantations, I am quite certain it would have brought him the money he needs and he need not have become beholden to other—people."

There was a pause before he said the last word, and Grania knew he had been about to say "Roderick Maigrin," then had changed his mind.

"Papa never made very much money out of the plantation," Grania said.

"That is because he grew too many different crops at the same time, instead of concentrating on one for which there was a demand."

Grania looked at the *Comte* in surprise, and he said with a smile:

"My plantations were very successful and I made a great deal of money."

"And you have looked at ours?"

"Yes; I was curious about them and wondered why your father should make himself dependent on his friends and neglect what could be a considerable source of income."

"I have always been told that the French were practical, and yet somehow you do not look like a businessman."

"I am, as you say, practical," the *Comte* replied, "and when my father died and I took over our plantations in Martinique, I was determined to make a success of them."

"And now you have lost them," Grania said. "It is too cruel that this should happen and I am so sorry for you."

"I will get them back. One day they will be mine again."

"In the meantime, please help us with ours."

"I want to, for your sake," the *Comte* answered, "but you must know it is impossible. All I can suggest is that you persuade your father to concentrate on growing nutmegs. They do well here, better than in other islands, and there is always a demand for them all over the world, as there has been since the beginning of time."

"I think Papa finds the nutmegs unattractive because they take so long to bear fruit."

The *Comte* nodded.

"That is true—eight to nine years. But they increase in yield until they are about thirty years old, and the average crop may be three to four thousand nuts per tree every year."

"I had no idea it was so much!" Grania exclaimed.

"What is more, they produce two main crops," the *Comte* went on. "You have quite a number of trees already, although unfortunately they are crowded by other fruits, and of course the undergrowth is restricting and stunting them."

He paused, then as he realised that Grania was listening to him raptly, he said:

"Forgive me, I am lecturing you. But quite frankly it

distresses me to see good land and what could be good crops wasted unnecessarily."

"I wish you could talk to Papa like that."

"I doubt if he would listen to me," the *Comte* replied wryly, "but perhaps you can talk to whoever runs the estate for your father."

"That was Abe, but Papa took him away because he could not be without him."

The *Comte* said nothing and there was silence between them.

Then Grania gave an exasperated little sigh.

"You are making me feel helpless and it is too big a problem for me."

"Of course it is, and it is unfair of me to talk to you like this. You should be enjoying life at your age and finding it all exciting and beautiful. Why should you have to worry about land that is unproductive and pirates who make use of your home when it is empty?"

The *Comte* was speaking in a low voice, as if he was talking to himself, and Grania laughed.

"I find pirates very exciting, and one day it will be a story to tell my children and my grandchildren, and they will think I was very adventurous."

She spoke lightly, as she might have spoken to her father or mother.

Then as she met the Frenchman's eyes she knew that if she had children they would be Roderick Maigrin's, and she wanted to scream at the very idea of it.

Instead, because of the way the *Comte* was looking at her, she felt the colour rise slowly in her cheeks, and her heart began to beat in a very strange manner.

Then there was the sound of voices and they were both very still as they listened.

"It is Abe!" Grania cried in a tone of relief.

Jumping up from her chair, she ran across the room and as she reached the Hall she called out:

"Abe! Abe!"

He came from the kitchen-quarters, followed by the French servant.

"What have you discovered?" Grania asked.

"Things very bad, Lady," Abe replied.

Then before he could say any more the French servant went to the side of the *Comte*, who had followed Grania from the Drawing-Room, and burst into a flood of such quick French that it was impossible for her to follow what he said.

Only when he had ceased speaking did she ask nervously:

"What . . . has happened?"

"It sounds bad," the *Comte* replied. "At the same time as the rebellion started in Grenville, Charlotte Town was attacked by another band of insurgents."

Grania gave a little cry of horror.

Charlotte Town, which was on the west side of the island only a little way above St. George's, was a place she knew well.

"Many lives have been lost," the *Comte* went on, "and a number of British inhabitants have been taken prisoner."

"Do they know who?"

The *Comte* questioned the Frenchman, but he shook his head.

Abe obviously understood what he had asked, for he said:

"Dr. John Hay prisoner."

"Oh no!" Grania exclaimed.

"Doctor and Rector of Charlotte Town taken Belvedere," Abe went on.

"Why Belvedere?" Grania questioned.

"That is where Redon has made his headquarters," the *Comte* replied. "The prisoners from Grenville have also been taken there."

Grania clasped her hands together.

"What shall we do?" she asked. "And is there any news of Papa?"

Abe shook his head.

"No, Lady, I send boy find out if Master coming."

The French servant then said a great deal more, and when he finished the *Comte* explained:

"There is no sign of any trouble so far in St. George's,

which is where the British soldiers are, so I think for
the moment you are safe, and when your father joins
you you will not be unprotected."

Grania did not say anything, she only looked at him,
and after a moment he added, as if she had asked the
question:

"Until your father arrives, I will stay in the harbour."

"Thank you."

She barely breathed the words beneath her breath,
but the expression in her eyes was very revealing.

"And now," the *Comte* said, "as Abe has had no
opportunity to cook luncheon for you and I believe like
me you are beginning to feel hungry, may I invite you to
what will be a simple meal aboard my ship?"

Grania's smile seemed to light up her whole face.

"You know I would like that."

The *Comte* gave his servant some instructions and he
left hurriedly by the front door, running across the
garden towards the harbour.

Grania drew Abe to one side.

"Listen, Abe," she said, "I am safe with *Monsieur*
Beaufort. He is not really a pirate but a refugee from
Martinique."

"Know that, Lady."

"You did not tell me!" Grania said reproachfully.

"Not expect him here."

Grania looked at him sharply.

"You knew that he had . . . come here before?"

There was a little pause and she knew that Abe
debated whether he should tell her the truth. Then he
answered:

"Yes, Lady, he come, not do no harm. Fine man!
While here he pay for what he take to ship."

"Pay for what?"

"Pigs, chickens, turkeys."

Grania laughed.

There was a remarkable difference between a pirate
who paid for what he requisitioned and other pirates
like Will Wilken who stole what they wanted and killed
if they were interfered with.

"You and I trust *Monsieur,* Abe," she said, "but Papa might be angry. Come and tell me if he is coming while I am aboard the ship so that I can be here in the house when he arrives."

She knew Abe would understand that he was to station two of their slaves to watch the road and the path through the forest.

She was not really afraid of what her father's reaction would be, but rather of Roderick Maigrin's if he was with him.

She was quite certain that he would shoot first and ask questions afterwards, and she thought that if she was instrumental in causing the *Comte* to be killed or wounded she would never forgive herself.

"Not worry, Lady," Abe said. "When Master come we ready."

"Thank you, Abe."

Because it was much hotter now than it had been earlier in the morning, she went upstairs to collect one of her new sunshades which she had brought back with her from London.

She came downstairs again to find the *Comte* waiting for her in the Hall. She felt like a child who was being taken on an unexpected treat, and she had the idea that he felt the same.

Without speaking they walked out onto the verandah, and when they started to descend the wooden steps which were slightly rickety as they needed repairing, the *Comte* put out his hand to help her.

Grania put her hand into his and as he took it she felt again that strange vibration that she had felt before, only this time it was more insistent.

His fingers closed over hers, and when the steps ended he still held her hand.

"I am looking forward to having a French luncheon," she said.

"I am afraid you have not given me enough time to prepare what I should like to offer you," the *Comte* replied, "but Henri, who has been with me for several years, will do his best."

"I also want to see the rest of your ship. How long have you had it, and did you build it yourself?"

The *Comte* gave a little laugh.

"I stole it!"

Grania waited for an explanation and he said:

"When the English invaded Martinique I knew that I must leave and I intended to do so in my own yacht. But when I went down to the harbour I saw the ship which you have already seen lying at anchor, and as I looked at it a friend who was with me said:

"'It is sad that the man whose company owns that ship is in Europe at the moment. It is too good a vessel to fall into the hands of the English.'"

"So you agreed with him and took it?"

"It seemed the proper thing to do."

"I think it was very sensible and practical, which are two things you like to be."

Yes, of course," he said, "and it meant that I could bring more people with me than I could have done otherwise, and I also transported a great amount of my furniture and my family paintings to a place where they will be safe until hostilities cease."

"Where is that?" Grania asked curiously.

"St. Martin," the *Comte* replied.

He said no more and she thought he did not wish to discuss it.

They walked in silence through the palm trees until when the ship was in sight she took her hand from his.

It was now very hot but there was a breeze from the sea.

The ship was still, but she noticed that the sails were no longer tied down but were ready to be raised at a moment's notice.

'Once he is gone I shall never see him again,' Grania thought.

She felt that these moments when she could be with the *Comte* were somehow very precious and something she would always remember.

They walked across the deck and down into the

cabin. The portholes were open and the sunshine came flooding in.

There was a table laid for two with a spotless white cloth and fresh flowers in the centre of it.

Besides the smell of bees'-wax there was also a delicious aroma of food, and before she could say anything the French servant who had been with Abe came into the cabin, carrying a tureen in his hand.

They sat down at the table and Jean, for that was what she had heard the *Comte* call him, filled two beautiful porcelain bowls.

There was crisp French bread to eat with the soup, and when Grania tasted it she knew it was made of stock, herbs, and other ingredients which she thought were fresh from the sea.

It was delicious and she realised that the aroma of it made her hungry, and she and the *Comte* both ate without speaking.

The servant brought wine that was golden like the sunshine and poured it into the glasses, and as they smiled at each other across the table Grania thought suddenly that she was happy.

For the first time since she had come home she was no longer worried or afraid.

When the soup was finished Jean brought them lobsters cooked with butter. They had obviously been swimming in the sea an hour or so earlier, and Grania suspected that they came from their own lobster-pots which had always been set in the bay when her mother was at home.

However, she asked no questions, but only ate eagerly because the lobsters were so tender and delicious and the salad which went with them was different from anything she had eaten while she was in London.

There was cheese and a bowl of fruit to follow the meal, but Grania could eat no more, so she and the *Comte* sat back and sipped their coffee.

Then at last the silence was broken, even though she thought they had been communicating with each other without words.

"If this is the life of a pirate," she said, "I think I shall become one."

"This is the moment," the *Comte* said, "when a pirate rests with his lady and forgets the danger, the uncertainty, and the discomfort of travelling over the face of the earth."

"At the same time, it must be exciting. You are free to go where you want, to take orders from nobody, and to live by your wits."

"As you have already said, I am sensible and practical," the *Comte* replied. "I want security, a wife and children, but that is something I can never have."

He spoke as if he was telling her something of infinite importance, but because she felt suddenly shy she did not look at him, but picked up her spoon to stir her coffee, although there was no need for it.

"A pirate's life is certainly no life for a woman," the *Comte* went on, as if he was following his own train of thought.

"But if there is no alternative?" Grania enquired.

"There is always an alternative to every situation," he replied firmly. "I could give up my piracy, but then I and the people who are with me would starve."

There was silence—a silence that seemed full of meaning—before the *Comte* said quickly:

"But why do we not talk of things that are interesting? Of books and paintings? Our different languages? And I have a great desire to hear you speak French."

"You may think I speak it badly," Grania replied in French.

"Your accent is perfect!" he exclaimed. "Who taught you?"

"My mother, and she was taught by a true Parisian."

"That is obvious."

"I also had lessons when I was at School in England," Grania explained, "although French was unpopular, and they were surprised that I should want to learn such a 'fiendish' language spoken by the people who were killing their own kin."

"I can understand that," the *Comte* said. "But even

though the English are at war with my country at the moment, I still want to learn to speak like an Englishman."

"Why?"

"Because it might come in useful."

"Your English is very good except for a few words which you mispronounce, and you sometimes put the stress on the wrong syllable."

The *Comte* smiled.

"Very well," he said. "When we are together I will correct you, and you will correct me. Is that a deal?"

"Yes, of course," Grania replied, "and to be fair we must divide our time together talking partly in English and partly in French, and there must be no cheating."

The *Comte* laughed. Then he said:

"It will be interesting to see who will be the better pupil, and I have the feeling, Grania, that because you are more sensitive than I am, you will take the prize."

Grania noticed that he called her by her Christian name, and once again he read her thoughts as he said:

"I cannot go on calling you 'My Lady' when already we know each other too well to be conventional."

"We only met this morning."

"That is not true," he replied. "I have known and admired you and talked to you for many nights, and your image has stayed with me during the day."

The way he spoke made her blush again and she felt the colour burning its way up to her eyes.

"You are very beautiful!" the *Comte* went on. "Far too beautiful for my peace of mind. If I were sensible and practical, as you tell me I am, I would sail away as soon as I set you ashore."

"No . . . please, you . . . promised you would . . . stay until my father . . . returned," Grania said quickly.

"I am being selfish and thinking of myself," the *Comte* replied.

"I am being selfish in doing the same," Grania admitted.

"Do you really want me to stay?"

"I am begging you to do so. I will go down on my knees, if that is what you want."

The *Comte* suddenly bent across the table and put out his hand. Slowly, because she felt shy, Grania put her hand in it.

"Now listen to me, Grania," he said. "I am a man without a home, without a future, an outlaw to both the French and the English. Let me go away while I am able to do so."

Grania's fingers tightened on his.

"I . . . cannot stop you . . . from going."

"But you are asking me to stay."

"I want you to. Please . . . I want you to. If you . . . go I shall be very . . . frightened."

Her eyes met his and it was impossible for her to look away. Then he said:

"As you have just reminded me, we only met a few hours ago."

"But . . . time does not . . . affect what I . . . feel about . . . you."

"And what do you feel?"

"That when I am with . . . you I am . . . safe and nothing can . . . hurt me."

"I wish that were true," he said.

"It is true. I know it is true!" Grania answered.

The *Comte* looked away from her down at her hand, then he raised it to his lips.

"Very well. I will stay, but when I do go you must not blame yourself and there must be no regrets."

"I promise . . . no regrets."

But as she spoke she had the feeling that it was a promise she would not be able to keep.

They sat talking for a little until Jean came in to take away the coffee, then the *Comte* said:

"Come and sit on the sofa and put up your feet. This is the time for a *siesta* and my crew will all be sleeping either on deck or below. I think it unlikely that we shall be disturbed, because your father will not travel in the heat of the day."

Grania knew this was true, and she walked to the sofa as the *Comte* suggested and sat back against the cushions, putting up her feet.

He pulled up an armchair to sit beside her and stretched out his long legs in their white stockings.

Grania smiled.

"Can this really be happening?" she asked. "I think both the French and the English would be very surprised if they could see us now."

"The English would certainly be very annoyed," the *Comte* replied. "They dislike pirates because they challenge their supremacy at sea, and that is something which is uncertain at the moment, with the rebellions both here and in Guadaloupe."

He paused before he went on:

"At the same time they held Martinique and a number of other islands, so undoubtedly the port of St. George's will sooner or later receive reinforcements."

Grania knew this was true, but she thought that until the solders arrived the rebels could do a great deal of damage.

Stories of how on other islands they had tortured their prisoners before they killed them had lost nothing in the telling.

She felt herself tremble as she imagined the indignities and perhaps the pain that Dr. Hay and the Anglican Rector might be suffering.

The *Comte* was watching her face.

"Forget it!" he said. "There is nothing you can do, and to keep thinking of such horrors is to bring them nearer and perhaps to make oneself more vulnerable."

Grania looked at him with interest.

"Do you believe that thought is transferable, and also strong enough to attract attention?"

"I assure you," the *Comte* replied, "I am not speaking of Voodoo or Black Magic when I say that the natives on Martinique know what is happening fifty miles away at the other end of the island long before it would be possible for a messenger to travel the distance with the information."

"You mean they are able to communicate with one another in a way that we have forgotten how to do?"

"I would never underestimate their powers."

"That is very interesting."

"As you are half-Irish it should be easy for you to understand," the *Comte* said.

"Yes, of course. Papa used to tell me stories about the powers of the Irish Sorcerers and how they could foretell the future. Of course I learnt about the Leprechauns when I was very small."

"Just as I learnt about the spirits that inhabit the mountains and forests in Martinique," the *Comte* said.

"Why could they not warn you before the English invaded the island?" Grania asked.

"Perhaps they tried to do so and we did not listen!" the *Comte* replied. "When you come to Martinique you can feel them, hear them, and perhaps see them."

"That is something I would love to do," Grania replied impulsively.

"You must trust to fate," the *Comte* answered, "which, as you know, has already brought you out of a very difficult situation, for which I am very grateful."

"As I am grateful to be here," Grania said. "When I rode through the forest I had the feeling I was escaping from a terrifying danger to something very different."

"What was that?"

She drew in her breath.

"It is what I feel when I am sitting here talking to you. I cannot . . . describe it exactly . . . but it makes me feel very . . . happy."

There was a moment's silence. Then the *Comte* said:

"That is all I want you to feel for the moment."

Chapter Four

The hours of heat passed slowly. Sometimes Grania and the *Comte* talked and sometimes they sat in silence as if they communicated with each other without words.

But she was aware that his eyes were on her face, and sometimes he made her feel shy in a way that was half-pleasure, half a strange embarrassment that seemed to have something magical about it.

Then there was the sound of footsteps overhead and the whistling of a man who was happy while he worked, and the *Comte* rose.

"I think I should take you back to the house," he said. "If your father is going to arrive he should be here in perhaps under an hour."

Grania knew that was the time it would take if her father came to her by road and not through the forest.

She wanted to stay longer and go on talking to the *Comte* or even just to be with him, but she could think of no viable excuse that did not sound intrusive, so reluctantly she rose from the sofa.

She had laid her head against a soft cushion, and now she patted her hair into place, feeling that she must be untidy, and looked round for a mirror.

"You look lovely!" the *Comte* said in his deep voice, and again she blushed.

He stood watching her before he said:

"I have to tell you how much it has meant to me to have you here and feel for the moment as if we have stepped out of time and are at peace with the world, or perhaps it would be better to say at peace with ourselves, for the world outside does not matter."

"That is what I think," Grania answered, but again it was hard to meet his eyes.

Reluctantly he turned to the cabin door and opened it.

"Come along," he said. "We must find out if there is any sign of your father, and you must be ready to talk to him and make him see your point of view."

Grania did not reply.

For the time being the *Comte* had given her a sense of security and, as he had said, peace, and it was hard to adjust her mind to what lay ahead, or even to feel menaced by Roderick Maigrin.

The *Comte* was with her, the sun was shining, the sea was vividly blue, and the palm trees were moving with an inexpressible grace in the warm wind.

When they were on deck she smiled at one of the men who was working at the ropes and he saluted her with a gesture that was very French and smiled back.

The *Comte* stopped.

"This is Pierre, my friend and neighbour when we lived in Martinique."

He spoke in French, and then he said to his friend:

"Let me present you, Pierre, to the beautiful lady whose hospitality we are enjoying because Secret Harbour belongs to her."

Pierre sprang to his feet, and when Grania put out her hand he raised her fingers to his lips.

"Enchanté, Mademoiselle."

She thought they might have been meeting in some Salon in Paris or London instead of on the deck of a pirate-ship.

She walked along the gang-plank and when the *Comte* joined her on the other side he said:

"Tomorrow, if I am still here, I would like you to meet the rest of my crew. It is best for them to remain anonymous, which is why I address them by their Christian names, but they are all men who have given up very different positions in life to save themselves from coming under the harsh jurisdiction of the English."

"Are we so harsh when we are in that position?" Grania asked.

"All conquerors seem intolerable to those who are conquered."

The *Comte* spoke roughly and for a moment Grania thought that he was hating her because she was an enemy.

Without meaning to she looked at him pleadingly, and he said:

"Forgive me, I am trying not to be bitter, and most of all to think not of myself but of you."

"You know I want you to do that," Grania said in a low voice.

But perceptively she knew that what he resented at the moment was that because their two countries were at war he could not offer her the safety of his estate in Martinique and they could not meet as ordinary people of different nationalities might do.

They moved through the thickness of the shrubs and pine trees until the house was in sight, then Grania stopped.

Everything was very quiet and she was certain that her father had not returned home.

Abe would have warned her if he had been sighted before he arrived.

At the same time, because the *Comte* was with her she had to be careful and make sure that she was not taking him into danger.

She thought for a moment that he would leave her and return to his ship, but instead when she moved forward again he kept beside her and they walked up the steps to the verandah and in through the open door.

It was then that she heard Abe talking to somebody in the kitchen, and she called his name.

"Abe!"

He came to her instantly, and she saw that he was smiling and that all was well.

"Good news, Lady,"

Introducing the Romantic World of Barbara Cartland Fragrances

A world of rare and exotic perfumes…
Inspired by the intensely romantic raptures
of love in every Barbara Cartland novel.

Experience the World of Barbara Cartland Fragrances

Awaken the romantic in your soul. With the
mysteriously beautiful perfumes of romance inspired
by Barbara Cartland. There's a heady floral bouquet
called *The Heart Triumphant,* an exotic Oriental essence
named *Moments of Love* and *Love Wins,* a tantalizing
woodsy floral. Each of the three, blended with the
poetry and promise of love. For every woman who has
ever yearned to love. Yesterday, today and especially
tomorrow!

Available at fragrance counters everywhere.

Helena Rubinstein®

"Of the Master?"

"No. No news from Maigrin House, but Momma Mabel come back."

Grania gave a little exclamation of delight. Then she asked:

"To stay? To work?"

"Yes, Lady. Very glad be back."

"That is splendid!"

She turned to the *Comte* and asked:

"Would you, *Monsieur*, do me the honour of dining here with me tonight? I cannot promise you a meal cooked by a French Chef, but my mother always thought that Momma Mabel was the best cook on the island."

The *Comte* bowed.

"*Merci, Mademoiselle*, I have much pleasure in accepting your most gracious invitation."

Grania gave a little laugh of delight.

"Shall we dine at seven-thirty?"

"I will not be late."

The *Comte* bowed again, then turned and walked back the way they had come.

She watched him go until he was out of sight, then she said to Abe:

"Let us have a dinner-party the way we used to do it when Mama was here, with the candelabra on the table and all the silver. Have we any wine?"

"One bottle, Lady," Abe answered. "I hide from Master."

Grania smiled.

When they had some really good wine her mother had always kept a few bottles hidden for special occasions. Otherwise her father would drink it indiscriminately and share it with anybody who came to the house, whatever their status in life.

Now she was glad she had what she was sure was a good claret to offer the *Comte*.

"Make a fruit drink for before dinner," she said, "and of course coffee afterwards. I will go speak to Momma Mabel."

She went to the kitchen, and as she expected Mom-

ma Mabel's huge figure and wide smile seemed to fill
the whole place.

She was an enormously fat woman, but actually she
herself ate very little.

What she could do was to cook in a way which had
made everybody on the island value the invitations they
received to Secret Harbour.

Grania remembered the Governor complaining that
they could never find anybody to cook as well as
Momma Mabel, and she knew that her mother had
suspected that he tried to entice her away with higher
wages than she was receiving at Secret Harbour.

But Momma Mabel, like many of the other servants
on the estate when her mother had been alive, thought
of herself as part of the family.

As long as the servants had enough to eat, whether
they received high or low wages or none at all was
immaterial.

Grania talked to Momma Mabel in the kitchen for
some time, then went to find Abe, and as she expected
he was cleaning the silver.

She watched him for a moment, then said in a low
voice:

"If the Master returns you must warn *Monsieur* that
he must not come."

Abe thought this over before he nodded and said:

"'Morrow Bella come back."

"I thought she must have gone away."

"She not far."

Bella was the maid who had looked after Grania since
she was small and when she grew older had made all
her gowns.

The Countess had taught her all the arts of being a
lady's-maid, and Grania knew that when Bella returned
she would be looked after and cosseted, and her clothes
from London would last far longer than they would
have done otherwise.

Then she thought that she was being over-optimistic
and her father would make her go back to Maigrin

House and marry its owner, and Bella would not go with her.

Then she told herself that she must believe that when her father did arrive she would somehow convince him that she could not marry Roderick Maigrin and that if they organised the plantation properly there would be enough money for them to live here quietly and be happy, however much they might miss her mother.

"Please . . . God, make him . . . listen to me," she prayed. "Please . . . please . . ."

She felt that her prayer wended its way towards the Heavens, and because she wanted to pray and also to look her best for her dinner-party she went upstairs to her bedroom.

Her trunks had not been unpacked and she knew Abe was wise to leave them for Bella.

Nevertheless, she searched until she found one of the prettiest gowns she owned.

It was one her mother had had made for her just before she grew ill, and although she was still ostensibly at School, Grania was sometimes allowed to dine with her mother's friends when there was a small party.

She held the gown up, shaking the creases out of the full skirt and knowing that the soft bodice with its small puffed sleeves was very becoming.

'I wonder if he will admire me,' she thought.

* * *

She was not disappointed when she saw the expression in the *Comte*'s eyes when he entered the Salon where she was waiting for him.

Although it was not yet dark she had lit some of the candles, and as he came in through the door she drew in her breath because he looked so magnificent.

She thought that if he was smart and very elegant in his day-clothes, in black satin knee-breeches and silk stockings with a long-tailed evening-coat and a frilled cravat no man could look more attractive.

If she found it difficult to find the words with which to greet him, it seemed as if the *Comte* felt the same.

For a moment they just stood looking at each other. Then as he walked towards her she felt almost as if he were enveloped with a light that came from within him.

It radiated out so that instinctively she wished to draw nearer and make herself a part of him.

"*Bon soir,* Grania."

"*Bon soir, Monsieur le Comte!*"

"And now let us say it in English," he said. "Good-evening, Grania! You look very beautiful!"

"Good-evening!" she answered.

She wanted to call him by his Christian name but the word would not come to her lips.

Instead, because she was shy she said quickly:

"I hope the dinner will not disappoint you."

"Nothing could disappoint me tonight."

She looked up at him and thought that in the light from the candles his eyes held a very strange expression and that they were saying something to her which she did not understand.

Then Abe came in with a fruit drink which also contained rum and just a touch of nutmeg sprinkled on top of the glass.

Grania took it from the silver tray, then once again it was difficult to find anything to say, and yet there was so much unsaid, and she felt despairingly that there would be no time to say it all.

They ate dinner in the Dining-Room which her mother had decorated with very pale green walls and green curtains so that it was as if one were outside in the garden.

The candles in the silver candelabra lit the table, and as dusk came and the shadows deepened it was a little island of light on which there were only two people and nothing else encroached.

The dinner was delicious, although afterwards Grania could never remember what she had eaten.

The *Comte* approved of the claret, although he drank it absentmindedly, his eyes on Grania.

"Tell me about your house in Martinique," she said.

As if he thought he must make an effort to talk, he told her how his father had built it and how he had employed an architect who had actually come from France to make it one of the finest houses on the island.

"There is one consolation," the *Comte* said. "I expected it, and I subsequently learnt that the English have made it their Headquarters, which means it will not be damaged or deliberately burnt as some of the other planters' houses have been."

"I am so glad."

"And so am I. One day I will be able to show it to you, and you will see how comfortable the French can make themselves even when they are far from their native land."

"What about your properties in France?"

The *Comte* shrugged his shoulders.

"I am hoping the Revolution will not have affected the South in the same way as it has the North. As Vence is a little, fortified city, perhaps it will escape."

"I hope so, for your sake," Grania said softly.

"Whatever happens, however," the *Comte* said, "I shall never return to France except for a visit. I have made Martinique my home just as my father did and I shall wait until it becomes mine again."

His voice deepened as he finished:

"Then I shall work to restore it to its former glory and make it a heritage for my children—if I have any."

There was a pause before the last few words, and because they were so closely attuned to each other Grania felt that he was saying that if he could not have children with her, he would remain unmarried.

Even as she thought of it she told herself that she was being absurd.

Marriages for Frenchmen were arranged almost from the time they were born, and it was only surprising that the *Comte* was not married already.

When he did, he would choose a Frenchwoman whose family equalled his own, and it would be almost impossible for him to take a wife of another nationality.

Her mother had often told her how proud the French were, especially the ancient families, and how those who had been guillotined had gone in the tumbrils with their heads held high, scornfully contemptuous of those who executed them.

Suddenly Grania felt insignificant and of no importance.

How could the daughter of a drunken and impecunious Irish Peer stand beside a man whose ancestors could doubtless trade their lineage back to Charlemagne?

She looked down at her plate, conscious for the first time that the paint was peeling from the walls, the curtains which should have been replaced years ago were ragged, and the carpet on the floor was threadbare.

To the eyes of a stranger the whole place must look, she thought, dilapidated, neglected, and poverty-stricken, and she was glad that the shadows hid what she felt was her own humiliation.

Dinner was over and the *Comte* pushed back his chair.

"We have finished. Shall we go into the Salon?"

"Yes, of course," Grania said quickly. "I should have suggested it."

She moved ahead, and when they entered the Drawing-Room the *Comte* shut the door behind them and walked very slowly to where Grania was standing by the sofa, feeling uncertain and unsure of herself, her eyes very large in her small face.

He came to her side and stood looking at her for a long time, and she waited, wondering what he was going to say, and yet afraid to ask what he was thinking.

Finally he said:

"I am leaving now. I am going back to my ship, and tomorrow at dawn we shall set sail."

She gave a little cry.

"Why? Why? You . . . said you would . . . stay!"

"I cannot do so."

"But . . . why?"

"I think you are woman enough to know the reason," he said, "without my having to explain."

Her eyes widened and he went on:

"You are very young, but you are old enough to know that one cannot play with fire and not be burnt. I have to go before I hurt you and before I hurt myself more than I have done already."

Grania clasped her hands together, but she could not speak, and he said:

"I fell in love with your painting when I first saw it, and I dare not tell you what I feel for you now, because it would be unfair."

"Un . . . fair?" Grania barely murmured.

"I have nothing to offer you, as well you know, and when I have gone you will forget me."

"That . . . will be . . . impossible."

"You think that now," the *Comte* said, "but time is a great healer, and we must both forget, not only for your sake but also for mine."

"Please . . . please . . ."

"No, Grania!" he said. "There is nothing either of us can do about the position in which we find ourselves. You are everything that a man could dream of and thinks he will never find. But you are not for me."

He put out his hand and took Grania's in his.

For a moment he stood looking down at it as if it were a precious jewel. Then slowly and with an indescribable grace he bent his head and kissed first the top of her hand and then, turning it over, the palm.

She felt a sensation like a streak of lightning flash through her, followed by a warm weakness which made her long to melt into him and become part of him.

Then her hand was freed and he walked towards the door.

"Good-bye, my love," he said very quietly. "God keep and protect you."

She gave a little cry, then the door was shut and she heard his footsteps crossing the verandah and going down the steps into the garden.

Then she knew that this was the end and there was nothing she could say or do to prevent it. . . .

* * *

A long time later Grania slipped into bed, and thought as she did so that this was where he had slept last night.

Abe had changed the sheets and they were cool and smooth, but she felt as if the impression of the *Comte's* body was still on them and the vibrations that had always passed from him to her were there. So it was almost as if she lay in his arms.

She could not cry, but she wanted to. Instead, there was a stone in her breast that seemed to grow heavier and heavier with every minute that passed.

"I have lost him! I have lost him!" she said to herself, and she knew there was nothing she could do about it.

She closed her eyes and went over the day hour by hour, minute by minute, remembering the things they had said to each other, what she had felt, then finally the feelings he had evoked in her when he had kissed her hand.

She pressed her lips to her own palm, trying to remember an ecstasy that had been so swift that it was hard to believe it had happened.

She wondered what he had felt. Had it been the same?

Although she was very ignorant about men and love, she was sure that he could not evoke such a response in her without feeling the same himself.

"I love him! I love him!"

The words seemed to repeat themselves over and over again in her mind, and she wished that she could die, that the world would come to an end and there would be no tomorrow.

She must have dozed a little, for suddenly the door burst open with a resounding crash and she gave a cry of fright as she woke and sat up in bed.

There was a light in her eyes and for a moment she could not see what was happening; then standing in the doorway, holding a lantern in his hand, she saw Roderick Maigrin!

For a moment Grania felt that she must be dreaming and it could not be true that he was there, big and solid with his legs apart as if he balanced himself, his face crimson in the light of the lantern, his blood-shot eyes black and menacing as he glared at her.

"What the devil do you think you're doing," he asked in a furious voice, "running away like that? I've come to fetch you back."

For a moment it was impossible for Grania to reply. Then in a voice that did not sound like her own she asked:

"Wh-where is . . . Papa?"

"Your father was not capable of making the journey," Roderick Maigrin replied, "so I've come in his place, and a great deal of trouble you've put me to, young lady!"

Grania managed to straighten her back before she said in a voice that was clearer:

"I am not coming . . . back to your . . . house. I want Papa to . . . come here."

"Your father will do nothing of the sort!"

He walked farther into the room to stand at the end of the bed, holding on to the brass knob of the bed-rail with one hand.

"If you hadn't been such a little fool as to run away in that cowardly manner," he said aggressively, "you would have learnt that I have dealt with the rebels who I suppose frightened you, and there will be no more rebellions on my estate."

"How can . . . you be . . . sure?" Grania asked, because it seemed the obvious question.

"I am sure," Roderick Maigrin replied, "because I made damned certain by killing the ring-leaders. They won't be able to spread any further sedition amongst my slaves!"

"You . . . killed them?"

"I shot them there and then, before they had a chance to do any more damage."

He boasted of it in a manner which told Grania that he had enjoyed the killings, and she was sure without asking that the men he had shot had been unarmed.

She wondered how she could make him leave.

Then as she felt for words, she saw the way he was looking at her and became uncomfortably conscious of the transparency of her thin nightgown and the fact that she was covered only by a sheet.

As instinctively she shrank back against the pillows, he laughed the low, lewd laugh of a man who was very sure of himself.

"You'll look damned attractive," he said, "when I've taught you to behave like a woman. Now hurry up and get dressed. I've a carriage waiting for you outside, although after the way you've behaved I ought to make you walk."

"You . . . mean for me to . . . come back with you now . . . at this moment?" Grania asked, thinking she could not understand what he was saying.

"With the moonlight to guide us it'll be a romantic drive," Roderick Maigrin said jeeringly, "and I've a Parson waiting to marry us tomorrow morning."

Grania gave a little cry of horror.

"I will not . . . marry you! I will not . . . come! I . . . refuse! Do you understand? I refuse!"

He laughed.

"So that's your attitude! I suppose, Miss High-and-Mighty, you think I'm not good enough for you. Well, that's where you're mistaken! If I hadn't bailed your drunken father out of debt, he'd be in prison. Get that into your head!"

He paused for a moment before his eyes narrowed and he said:

"If you are not prepared to accompany me dressed, I'll take you back as you are and enjoy doing it!"

It was a threat which he looked prepared to put into operation, for he moved round the bed-post towards her, and she gave a cry of sheer terror.

Then there was a knock on the open door and Roderick Maigrin turned his head.

Abe was standing there.

He carried a glass on a silver tray, and his face was impassive as he walked forward to say:

"You like drink, Sir."

"I would!" Roderick Maigrin replied. "But it's just like your damned impertinence to follow me up the stairs!"

He took the glass from the tray, then as Abe did not move he said:

"I suppose I have you to thank for helping your Mistress to run away in that blasted foolish fashion! I'll have you whipped in the morning for not informing your Master where you were going."

"I try wake Master, Sir," Abe said, "not move him."

Roderick Maigrin did not answer.

He was eagerly drinking the rum punch that Abe had brought him, pouring it down his throat as if it were water.

He finished the glass, then set it down with a bang on the silver salver that Abe still held in his hand.

"Get me another!" he said. "And while I'm drinking it you can take your Mistress's trunks downstairs and put them on my carriage."

He paused before he added:

"She's coming back with me. You can follow and bring your Master's horses with you. You'll neither of you be coming back here."

"Yes, Sir," Abe said, and turned to walk from the room.

Grania wanted to call out to him not to leave her, but she knew that if Roderick Maigrin whipped or killed Abe there would be nothing she could do about it.

However, it seemed that Abe's appearance had diverted Maigrin's worst attentions from her, for he wiped his lips with the back of his hand and said:

"Hurry up and get dressed or you will find I'm not joking when I say I'll take you as you are. When you're my wife you'll be obedient, or you'll find it a painful experience to defy me."

As he spoke he walked towards the door.

Only as he reached it did he realise that if he took the lantern with him Grania would be left in the dark.

He put it down noisily on top of the chest-of-drawers, then holding on to the bannisters he started to go down the stairs, shouting as he did so:

"Light the candles, you lazy slave! How do you expect me to find my way in the dark?"

Grania felt as if she were paralysed into immobility, and she thought wildly that there was only one person who could save her now, not only from being taken back to Maigrin House but from being married in the morning.

Even as she thought of the *Comte* she knew it was impossible to reach him.

The house had been built with only one staircase since the servants slept outside in cabins, one to each family.

The only way of escape would be through the Hall, and whether Roderick Maigrin sat in the Dining-Room or the Drawing-Room he would see her pass and undoubtedly follow her.

Then he would not only find out where she was going, but she would also have betrayed the *Comte* to a man who she was certain would be vindictive in a manner that might end in the death of all those who were on his ship.

"What . . . can I . . . do? What can . . . I do?" Grania asked herself frantically.

Because there was no alternative, she got out of bed.

She did not underestimate Roderick Maigrin's threat that he would take her dressed as she was, and she realised that he would positively delight in humiliating her and in proving his mastery over her and over her father.

Tomorrow she would be married to such a man!

When she thought of it she knew that she could never marry him. If that was the fate that was waiting for her, she would kill herself before she actually became his wife.

And if she did kill herself he would probably still go

on helping her father because he was an Earl, and his threat of letting him go to prison would never be put into operation while he still had some use for him socially.

"I will die!" Grania told herself firmly, and wondered how she could do it.

Slowly, because time was passing, she began to dress.

She had just taken from the wardrobe the gown she had worn that day and slipped it over her head when Abe appeared.

He had walked so quietly up the stairs that she had not heard him, and now as he came into the room she looked at him as she had done when as a child she had gone to him in trouble.

"Abe . . . Abe!" she murmured. "What . . . can I . . . do?"

Abe put his finger to his lips, then as he crossed the room to close one of her trunks and strap it up he said in a whisper she could barely hear:

"Wait here, Lady, 'til I fetch you."

Grania looked at him in surprise, wondering what he meant.

Then he picked up her trunk, put it on his shoulder, and walked down the stairs, making no effort to walk quietly but seeming to accentuate the noise of his footsteps.

He must have passed through the Hall, then a few minutes later Grania heard him say in his quiet, respectful voice:

"Another drink, Sir?"

"Give it to me and get on with the luggage!" Roderick Maigrin snarled, and Grania knew he was sitting just inside the Drawing-Room door.

"Three more trunks, Sir."

"Tell your Mistress to come down and talk to me. I find it boring sitting here alone."

"Not ready, Sir," Abe replied, and by this time he was halfway up the stairs.

He closed a second trunk and took it down.

Once again Grania heard him give Mr. Maigrin another drink.

She thought that perhaps Momma Mabel was preparing them in the kitchen, but there was no sound of their voices and Abe came upstairs again. This time he was not empty-handed.

He was carrying a large washing-basket in which clothes after they had been washed were taken out to be attached to the line on which they would dry.

Grania looked at him in surprise as Abe set it down on the floor and without speaking motioned her to get inside it.

She understood, and, crouching down in the basket, she waited while he fetched a sheet from the bed and put it over her, tucking it down round her without speaking.

Picking up the basket by its two handles, he started down the stairs.

Now Grania's heart was beating frantically as she knew that even though he had had a lot to drink, there was every chance of Roderick Maigrin thinking it strange that her clothes which had come from London should be in an open washing-basket.

However, she was aware that there was nothing else in the house in which she could be carried and Abe had taken a chance on the fact that Mr. Maigrin would not be expecting her to escape in such an undignified manner.

Abe reached the last step of the stairs.

Now he was walking across the Hall and passing the open door of the Drawing-Room.

Through the open wicker-work Grania could see the lights from several candles and she thought she could vaguely distinguish the large body of the man she loathed sprawled in one of her mother's comfortable armchairs, a glass in his hand.

She was not sure if she really saw this with her eyes or with her imagination.

Then Abe had passed the door and was walking down the passage to the kitchen and she held her breath, just in case at the very last moment she would hear Roderick Maigrin shouting at them to stop.

But Abe walked on, and now he carried her out through the back door and, still not stopping, moved into the thickness of the bougainvillaea bushes which grew right up to the walls of the house.

Only as he put the basket down on the ground did Grania realise that he had rescued her and now she could reach the *Comte* without Roderick Maigrin knowing where she had gone.

Abe pulled off the sheet which had covered her and in the moonlight Grania could see his eyes looking at her anxiously.

"Thank you, Abe," she whispered. "I will go to the ship."

Abe nodded and said:

"Bring trunks later."

As he spoke he pointed, and Grania saw that the two trunks he had already brought downstairs were hidden under the bushes, where it would be difficult for anybody who was unsuspecting to see them.

"Be careful," she warned, and he smiled.

Then as the terror which enveloped her swept over her like a tidal wave, she started to run frantically, wildly, as if Roderick Maigrin were already pursuing her down through the bushes and trees towards the harbour.

Chapter Five

Although it was dark between the trees Grania could not stop running. Then suddenly she bumped into something, and realising at once that it was human, she gave a little scream of fear.

But even as it left her lips she knew who it was.

"Save . . . me! Save . . . me!" she begged frantically, speaking only in a whisper for fear her voice would be overheard.

"What has happened? What has upset you?" the *Comte* asked.

For a moment Grania was too breathless to speak.

She was only aware that she was close to the *Comte*, and without really thinking of what she was doing she moved closer, still hiding her face against his shoulder.

Slowly, almost as if he tried to prevent himself from doing so, he put his arms round her.

To feel him holding her was an indescribable comfort and after a moment she managed to say:

"He has . . . come to fetch me . . . away . . . I am to be . . . married tomorrow . . . and I thought I would . . . never escape."

"But you have," the *Comte* said. "My look-out saw lights in the windows of your house and I was coming to investigate in case something was wrong."

"Very . . . very wrong," Grania replied, "and I thought I could not . . . get away . . . but Abe . . . carried me out in a . . . washing-basket."

As she spoke she thought it ought to sound amusing, but she was still so frightened and so breathless from the speed at which she had run that what she said was almost incoherent.

"Is Maigrin in the house?" the *Comte* asked.

"He is . . . waiting for . . . me."

The *Comte* did not reply, he merely turned her round so that she faced in the direction of the ship, and with his arms round her shoulders he led her through the trees to the harbour.

Because he was with her and was actually touching her, she felt her agitation gradually subside.

At the same time, she felt too limp and weak to think for herself any longer.

As if he understood, when they reached the gangway the *Comte* steadied her on it, then walked behind her with his hands on her arms in case she lost her balance.

They stepped on deck and for a moment Grania thought there was no-one about.

Then she saw a man halfway up the mast and supposed he was the look-out of whom the *Comte* had spoken.

Now that she was on deck she turned to look back at the house and realised that the trees and shrubs made it completely invisible. Only the man on the mast could have seen the lights in the windows which had made him alert the *Comte*.

They went down the steps to the cabin and she saw that when this had happened he was already in bed.

The sheets were thrown back, and she saw now by the light of a lantern that he was wearing only a thin linen shirt open at the neck and dark pantaloons.

He stood looking at her and for the first time she was conscious of her own appearance and that her hair was hanging loosely over her shoulders. She had made no effort to tidy it when she had dressed on Roderick Maigrin's instructions.

The *Comte* did not speak and Grania said the first thing that came into her mind:

"I . . . I cannot . . . go back!"

"No, of course not. But where is your father?"

"He was not . . . well enough to . . . come with Mr. Maigrin."

She did not look at the *Comte* as she spoke, but they both knew it was because the Earl was drunk that he had stayed behind at Maigrin House.

"Sit down," the *Comte* said unexpectedly. "I want to talk to you."

Obediently and also gladly because her legs felt as if they could no longer support her, Grania sat down in one of the comfortable armchairs.

There were two lanterns hanging in the cabin and she saw that the portholes were covered by wooden shutters that she had not noticed earlier in the day, and she knew that no light could be seen from outside.

The *Comte* hesitated a moment. Then he said, still standing looking down at Grania:

"I want you to think seriously of what you are asking me to do."

She did not answer. She only looked at him apprehensively, afraid he would refuse.

"You are sure," he went on, "there is not somebody else on the island with whom you could hide from your father and who could also keep you safe from the rebels?"

"There is . . . nobody," Grania said simply.

"And nowhere on any other island where you could be with friends?"

Grania hung her head.

"I know I am being a . . . nuisance to you," she said, "and I have no . . . right to ask you to . . . protect me. But at the moment it is difficult to think of . . . anything except that I am . . . terribly afraid."

As she spoke she thought she was stating her feelings very badly, and what she really wanted to do was to beg the *Comte* to keep her with him.

Then she knew it was a very reprehensible way to behave when she had only just met him, and he had made it quite clear that she could have no part in his life.

Because she thought he must know what she was thinking, she looked up at him and said:

"I am . . . sorry . . . I am very . . . sorry to ask . . . this of you."

He smiled and she felt as if a dozen more lights illuminated the cabin.

"There is nothing to be sorry about from my point of view," he said, "but I am trying to think of yours."

He paused before he went on:

"You have your whole life in front of you, and if your mother had been alive you would have taken your place in London Society. It is hardly a reasonable alternative to be the only woman aboard a pirate-ship."

"But it is where . . . I want to . . . be," Grania said almost beneath her breath.

"Are you quite sure of that?"

"Quite . . . quite . . . sure."

She felt an irresistible impulse to rise and go close to him as she had been a few minutes before. She wanted his closeness, his strength, the feeling of security he gave her.

Then, because her yearning to do that was so intense that she felt the colour come into her face, she looked away from him shyly.

As if she had told him what he wanted to know, the Comte said:

"Very well. We will leave here at dawn."

"Do you mean that . . . do you really mean it?" Grania asked.

"God knows if I am doing the right thing," he answered, "but I have to protect you. That man is not fit to associate with any decent woman."

Grania gave an exclamation of horror.

"Suppose he . . . finds us? Suppose when he . . . realises I am not in the house he comes . . . here?"

"That is unlikely," the Comte said, "and if he does I will deal with him. But it will be impossible to sail before morning without a wind."

"He will not . . . suspect there is a ship in the . . . harbour," Grania said as if she was reassuring herself, "and if he does come this way, Abe will warn us."

"I am sure he will," the *Comte* agreed.

"When Mr. Maigrin has . . . gone, Abe will bring my . . . trunks from . . . where he has . . . hidden them."

"I will tell the man on watch to look out for him," the *Comte* said, then he went from the cabin.

When he had gone, Grania clasped her hands together and said a prayer of thankfulness.

"Thank You, God, for letting me stay with him! Thank You that the ship was here when I most needed it!"

She thought how terrifying it would have been if to escape from Roderick Maigrin she had had to run off into the jungle alone and hide amidst the tropical vegetation.

She had the feeling that if she had done so he would somehow have found her. Perhaps with dogs, perhaps instructing his own slaves to search.

"Thank You . . . God . . . thank You for the . . . *Comte*," she said as she heard his footsteps returning.

He came into the cabin and once again Grania resisted an impulse to run to him and hold on to him to make sure he was really there.

"There are still lights burning in the house," he said, "so I imagine that your unwelcome visitor has not left."

As he spoke there was a faint whistle from outside.

"I think that is to tell us that Abe is arriving," he said.

Grania jumped to her feet.

"I hope he is all right. I am terribly . . . afraid that when Mr. Maigrin finds me . . . gone he will vent his . . . rage on Abe."

She followed the *Comte* out on deck, carefully shutting the cabin door behind her.

However, it was quite easy to see by moonlight and when she walked over to the side of the ship she saw Abe walking along by the water's edge, carrying one of her trunks.

When he came on board she was waiting for him.

"What is happening, Abe?"

"Everything all right, Lady," Abe replied. "Mister Maigrin asleep."

"Asleep!" Grania exclaimed.

Abe grinned.

"Put little powder in last drink. He sleep now 'til morning. Wake with bad head!"

"That was clever of you, Abe."

"Very clever!" the *Comte* agreed.

"I bring luggage," Abe said. "You go 'way, not come back 'til safe."

"That is what I want to do," Grania replied, "but what about you? I am afraid Mr. Maigrin will whip you."

"I all right, Lady," Abe replied. "He not find me."

Grania knew there were many places on the island where Abe could hide, and she knew that however much her father needed him it would be impossible for him to face Roderick Maigrin's anger and the cruelty with which he treated all those who served him.

"I fetch other trunks," Abe said, "and Joseph take carriage."

Grania was surprised.

"Where will he take it?"

Abe's smile was very broad and she could see the flash of his white teeth in the moonlight.

"When Mister wake, he think you go Master. Joseph leave horses and come back."

"That is a brilliant idea!" Grania exclaimed. "And even if he thinks I am hiding, Mr. Maigrin will look for me near his own house."

Abe smiled with an almost childish delight. Then he said again:

"I fetch other trunk."

"Wait a minute," the *Comte* said. "I will send somebody with you."

He spoke to the man up on the mast, who slid down onto the deck. The *Comte* told him what to do and he followed Abe across the gang-plank.

The *Comte* picked up Grania's trunk and carried it towards the cabin.

She ran ahead to open the door for him, but when they were inside she said:

"I cannot take your cabin. There must be somewhere else I can sleep."

"This is where, as my guest, you *will* sleep," he said firmly, "and I hope you will be comfortable."

Grania gave a little laugh of sheer happiness.

"Very comfortable . . . and very safe," she said. "How can I thank you for being so kind to me?"

He did not answer, but as they looked at each other she had the feeling that he was telling her that he was as happy as she was and there was no need for them to express what they felt in words.

Because his expression made her feel shy, Grania said quickly:

"I must give Abe some money. I have some money with me which I put in one of my trunks."

She had hidden the money she had brought with her from England because she was afraid that her father would take it from her and she would be left penniless.

When her mother had become ill and then grown weaker and weaker, she had said to Grania:

"I want, dearest, to draw out from my Bank all the money I have left."

"Why should you want to do that, Mama?" Grania had enquired.

There had been a long pause, as if the Countess was considering what she should say.

Then, as if she felt it was a mistake to tell Grania anything but the truth, she had said:

"You must have some money of your own, which is not to be thrown away on the gaming-tables or the drink your father finds indispensable. It will not only pay for your trousseau when you marry, but you will be independent—if things go wrong!"

She had not elaborated on what she meant, and because her mother was weak Grania knew how important it was to do what she wanted and not ask too many questions.

"I understand, Mama. You do not have to explain to me. I will do exactly what you wish me to do."

She had gone to the Bank the same day and drawn out the few hundred pounds that her mother had left.

"Are you wise, My Lady," the Manager had asked, "to carry so much money about with you?"

"I will put it in a safe place," Grania had promised.

She knew he thought she was being reckless, but now it was a joy to know that she could give Abe enough to support himself and pay the old servants and the slaves who were still supposed to be in their employment although they had probably received no wages.

"Let me do that for you," the *Comte* said.

"Of course not," Grania replied. "I have my pride. Actually I have some money and this is the way I want to spend it."

As she spoke she thought that when her mother was speaking of her trousseau she had no idea that her daughter might have been married to the man she had always despised.

The *Comte* undid the straps of her trunk and opened it for her, and she found the money she sought at the bottom of it.

She counted out fifteen golden sovereigns, thinking that Abe would consider it a large sum and it would last him a long time.

The *Comte* had left the cabin, and after she had placed the money in a small bag which had also come from the Bank she went on deck to join him.

He was watching for Abe, and when he appeared with the Frenchman also carrying a trunk, Grania had the feeling that the *Comte* had been anxious just in case Roderick Maigrin had not been asleep and might have followed them.

The trunks were brought aboard and Grania took Abe to one side.

"Here is some money for you, Abe," she said. "It is for yourself and for anyone else on the plantation who you think has earned it."

She put the bag into his hand and went on:

"When Mr. Maigrin gives up looking for me, set the slaves to clear the undergrowth round the nutmeg trees. When things are better we will plant more of them and hope to have a crop that will make more money than we have had in the past."

"Good idea, Lady."

"Take care of the house, Abe, until I come back."

"You come back—Master miss you."

"Yes, of course I will," Grania answered, "but only when it is safe."

As she said the words she looked over her shoulder and saw that the *Comte* was not far away.

"How will we know when it is safe for us to return?" she asked.

"You will want news of your father," the *Comte* replied, "but we must be sure that the rebels have not taken St. George's as well as the other parts of the island."

"If safe, Sir," Abe said, "I leave sign."

"That is what I was going to suggest."

"If safe come here," Abe said as if he was thinking aloud, "I put white flag outside entrance."

"And if there is danger?" the *Comte* enquired.

"If rebels or Mister Maigrin in house, I leave black flag."

Grania knew the flags would be only white or dark rags tied to a stick, but the message nevertheless would be very clear.

She put out her hand to Abe, saying:

"Thank you, Abe, you have looked after me ever since I was a child, and I know you will not fail me now."

"You safe, Mister Beaufort, Lady."

He shook her hand and turned to leave.

"Please, Abe, take good care of yourself," Grania pleaded. "I cannot lose you."

His smile was very confident and she knew that in a way he was enjoying the excitement and even the danger of what they had just passed through.

Then as he disappeared amongst the pine trees the *Comte* said:

"You are now under my command, and I am going to give you your orders."

Grania gave a little laugh.

"Aye, aye, Sir! Or is that only what the English sailors say?"

"Tomorrow I will teach you what to say in French," the *Comte* replied, "but now you are to go to bed and sleep. I think you have been through enough dramatics for one night."

She smiled at him and he walked ahead of her to open the cabin door. The man who had fetched the trunks with Abe followed and put them tidily against one wall.

"Do you want me to open them now?" the *Comte* asked.

Grania shook her head.

"I have everything I need in the one you have opened already."

The *Comte* extinguished one of the lanterns which were hanging from the ceiling and lifted down the other to place it beside the bed.

He undid the little glass door so that it was easy for her to extinguish it.

"Is there anything else you want?"

"No, nothing," she replied, "and thank you. I am so happy to be here that I just want to keep saying 'thank you' over and over again."

"You can thank me tomorrow," the *Comte* said, "but now I think it important for you to rest. *Bonne nuit, Mademoiselle, dormez bien.*"

"*Bon soir, mon Capitaine,*" Grania replied.

Then she was alone.

* * *

When Grania awoke it was to feel the rolling of the ship and to hear the creaking of the boards, the straining of the wind in the sails, and somewhere far away in the distance the noise of voices and laughter.

For a moment she could not think where she was, then she remembered that she was at sea, far away from Roderick Maigrin and from the fear that had been like a stone in her breast.

"I am safe! I am safe!" she wanted to cry, and she knew she was happy because she was with the *Comte*.

She had gone to sleep very conscious that her head was on his pillow, that she lay on the mattress on which he had slept, and that she was covered by the sheet that had been his.

She felt close to him as she had felt when she had run into him in the darkness and hidden her face against his chest.

She was conscious then of the warmth of his body even before she had known the strength of his arms, and she felt that in her dreams he was still holding her.

She sat up in bed and pushed her hair back from her forehead.

She was sure that she had slept for a long time and it must be late, yet it did not matter if it was.

There was no Parson waiting for her, no Roderick Maigrin trying to touch her, no horrors lurking amongst the trees or in the house.

"I am safe!" Grania said again, and got out of bed.

By the time she was dressed she knew she was hungry. At the same time, she did not hurry.

She found a small mirror amongst her other things and took a long time brushing her hair and arranging it in the way she had worn it in London, which her mother had thought was very becoming.

Then she found a gown that was one of her prettiest, and only when the tiny mirror told her that she looked very elegant did she open the cabin door to the blinding sunshine.

The deck that had seemed deserted before was now full of activity.

There were men at the ropes, men climbing up and down the masts, and the sails were billowing out in the sea breeze.

The sea was dazzlingly blue and the gulls were whirling overhead and making a great deal of noise about it.

Grania stood looking round. She knew that she was looking for only one man, and when she saw him she felt her heart give a leap as if she had been afraid he would not be there.

He was at the wheel, and she thought that with his hands on the spokes, his head lifted as if he searched the far horizon, no man could look more handsome or more omnipotent, as if he were not only Captain of his ship but Master of everything he surveyed.

She would have gone towards him, but he saw her and gave the wheel over to another man and came walking towards her.

As he joined her she saw his eyes travel over her, and there was a faint smile on his lips as if he realised the trouble she had taken to make herself look attractive and was appreciative.

"I am so very late," Grania said, because she felt he was waiting for her to speak.

"It is almost midday," he replied. "Would you wait for luncheon, or would you like to have the breakfast you missed this morning?"

"I will wait," Grania replied, because she wished to stay with him.

He put his arm through hers and led her along the deck, stopping every few steps to introduce her in turn to men working at the ropes.

"This is Pierre, this is Jacques, this is André, and this is Leo."

Only later did Grania know that three of the men on board had been very rich when they left Martinique.

Two were planters in the same way that the *Comte* considered himself one and had owned a large number of slaves, and the third, Leo, was a Lawyer with the biggest practice in St. Pierre, the Capital of Martinique.

She was to learn that they showed their courage in the way they were never bitter about the fate that had swept their possessions from them, but merely optimistic that one day their fortunes would change and they would return home to claim what they had lost.

The rest of the men aboard were the personal servants of the *Comte* and his friends, together with several young clerks from Leo's office, all of whom were deeply grateful for the privilege of escaping with him when they might have been imprisoned or forced to work for their conquerors.

In the next two days while they were at sea, Grania learnt that it was not only a busy ship but a happy one.

From first thing in the morning until last thing at night the crew sang, whistled, and laughed amongst themselves as they worked.

None of the men were trained seamen, and the mere running of the ship required not only their intelligence but the use of muscles they had not employed before.

It appeared to Grania as if they made it a game, and she would lean over the rail of the poop-deck, watching them, listening to them singing and cracking jokes with one another and often tossing a coin to decide who would climb the tall raking spars to trim the sails.

She noticed that even amongst his friends the *Comte* appeared always to be in command, always the leader.

She had the feeling, and was sure she was not wrong, that they trusted him just as she did. He gave them a sense of safety, and without him they too would have been afraid.

She had thought when she went aboard the ship that she would be alone with the *Comte*, but this was something that did not happen.

Always there seemed to be so much for him to do, and too he appeared always to be looking out for danger.

Whenever the look-out reported a ship on the horizon they made off in another direction, and Grania was not certain at first whether this was something he would have done if she had not been on board.

She had also thought that they would have meals

together, but she learnt that the Comte's three friends always had dinner with him and when they were at sea luncheon was a meal through which everybody went on working.

Henri, the Chef, prepared cups of soup which the men drank as they performed their duties. There was also cheese *or pâté*, placed between long pieces of French bread which were sliced horizontally.

Grania ate like the others, either on deck or, when she was tired of the sunshine, alone in her cabin while she read a book.

She found the Comte's books not only interesting but also intriguing.

She had guessed that he would enjoy Rousseau and Voltaire, but she had not expected that he would have a large collection of poetry books, and English poetry at that, or that he would also have several religious books on the shelves.

"I suppose he is Catholic," she said to herself.

Perhaps it was due to the air or to the movement of the ship, or maybe it was because she was content and happy, that Grania slept in the Comte's bed deeply and dreamlessly, as if she were a child, to wake with a feeling of excitement because it was the beginning of another day.

Then late one afternoon, after the heat was over, they came in sight of St. Martin.

At dinner the previous night the Comte and his friends had told Grania that the smallest territory in the world was shared by two sovereign states.

"Why?" Grania had asked.

Leo, who was the Lawyer, laughed.

"According to legend," he said, "the Dutch and the French prisoners-of-war who had been brought to the island in 1648 to destroy the Spanish Fort and buildings came from their hiding-places after the Spanish had been routed, and they realised they had an island to share."

"By peaceful means," Jacques interposed.

"They had had enough of fighting," the *Comte* added, "and so the boundaries were decided by a walking contest."

Grania laughed.

"How can they have done that?"

"A Frenchman and a Dutchman," Leo explained, "started at the same spot and walked round the island in opposite directions, having agreed that the boundary line should be drawn straight across the island where they met."

"What a wonderful idea," Grania cried. "Why can they not do something so simple on the other islands?"

"Because the others are much larger," Leo replied. "The Frenchman's walking-pace was stimulated by wine, so that he went faster than the Dutchman, who was actually slowed down because he preferred his own Dutch gin."

All the men laughed, but Leo said:

"Whatever the origin of the boundary, the French and Dutch have lived in harmony ever since."

"That is what I call very, very sensible," Grania said.

For the first time since she had come aboard, the *Comte* stayed behind after his three friends had left the cabin.

Grania looked at him enquiringly and he said:

"I have something to suggest to you, but I am rather afraid you will not like it."

"What is it?" Grania asked apprehensively.

The *Comte* did not answer for a moment, and she realised he was looking at her hair.

"Is . . . anything wrong?"

"I was just thinking how beautiful you are," he said, "and it would certainly be wrong for me to change you in any way, but it is something which I think is important."

"What is it?"

"I have to think of you," the Comte said, "and not only your safety but also your reputation."

"In what way?"

"When we arrive at St. Martin, even though my

house is very isolated, you can well imagine that in the space of only twenty-one square miles everything is known and gossiped about."

Grania nodded.

"That is why I think you must change your identity."

"You mean . . . I must not be . . . English?"

"The French, even in St. Martin, are very patriotic."

"Then can I be French, like you?"

"That is of course what I would like you to be," the *Comte* replied, "and I thought I could introduce you as my cousin, *Mademoiselle* Gabrielle de Vence."

"I shall be delighted to be your cousin."

"There is one difficulty."

"What is that?"

"You do not look in the least French, but, if I may say so, very English."

"I always thought that I owe my eye-lashes, which are dark, to my Irish ancestry."

"But your hair, which is like sunshine, is as obvious as any Union Jack."

Grania laughed.

"I think I am insulted that you should think it is red, white, and blue!"

"What I am suggesting is that it should be a different colour," the *Comte* said quietly.

She looked at him in astonishment.

"Are you asking me to . . . dye my hair?"

"I have talked to Henri," he said, "and he has distilled what he calls a 'rinse' which is easily washed out when you wish to revert to your own nationality."

Grania looked doubtful, but the *Comte* went on:

"I promise you it is not black or anything unpleasant. It will just change the shining gold of your hair to something a little more ordinary—the colour that a Frenchwoman could easily own, although she would never, I am afraid, have a skin so clean and soft that it is like the petals of a camelia."

Grania gave a little smile.

"That sounds very poetic."

"I find it very difficult not to be when I am talking to

you. At the same time, Grania, as you have pointed out
before, the French are sensible and realistic, and that is
what we both must be."

"Yes . . . of course," she agreed.

But she was reluctant to dye her hair, feeling that
perhaps she would not look so attractive in the *Comte's*
eyes.

Henri came to the cabin to explain to her what she
must do, and first of all he dipped a tress of her hair in
a liquid he had in a jug, and she saw that it took away
the gold and darkened it considerably.

"No, no! I cannot do it!" she exclaimed.

He put down the small jug and brought another one
filled with fresh water, and, dipping her hair once
again, he swirled it round, then held it up.

The brown had vanished.

"That is very clever of you, Henri!" Grania cried.

"It is a very good dye," Henri said with delight.
"When there is no more war I will put it on the market
and make my fortune!"

"I am sure you will."

Henri explained to her that if they used a walnut
dye, or even one distilled from nutmegs, it would take
months to remove and the hair would have to grow out
before she was absolutely free of it.

"This is different," he said proudly, "and one day, you
see, *M'mselle*, everyone in Paris will be asking for
'Henri's Quick-Change Colour'!"

Grania laughed.

"I am delighted, Henri, to be the first to try it."

Henri brought a basin and towel and dyed her hair
for her.

When she looked at herself in a much larger mirror
than she had used before, she thought at first she
looked like a stranger and one she did not particularly
admire.

Then she knew that if her skin had seemed white
before, now it glowed like a pearl, and in a way she
thought that the darkness of her hair made her look
intriguing and perhaps a little mysterious.

She came on deck the next morning somewhat self-consciously, but the *Comte*'s friends had no inhibitions.

They complimented her so vociferously that she blushed and ran away from them! When she reached the *Comte*, who once again was at the steering-wheel, he smiled and said:

"I see I have a very pretty new relative! You will certainly embellish the annals of the *Comtes de Vence!*"

"I was afraid you might be ashamed of me."

He merely smiled at her and there was a look in his eyes which told her far better than words that she had not lost his admiration, which was all she wanted to know.

She stayed beside him and soon he realised that she wanted him to show her how to steer the ship.

It was not so much the excitement of doing something that gave her a feeling of power, but that to make certain she did it properly he stood behind her at the wheel, putting his hands above hers on the spokes.

She could feel the closeness of his body, and as they looked out towards the horizon she felt that they were sailing over the edge of the world and the past was left behind them.

It was only when the *Comte* had walked away from her that she suddenly felt alone.

She had been so happy these past days and she was afraid that when they reached St. Martin things would change.

She was watching him on the deck below and for a moment she lost control of the wheel and the ship keeled over in the breeze.

Instantly one of the men came to help her set it to rights.

She gave the wheel to him and walked down onto the deck to follow the *Comte*.

It was then that she knew quite suddenly that she wanted to be near him, that she wanted to feel him close to her, and that it was an agony when he was away.

"What is the matter with me?" she asked herself. "How can I feel like this?"

Then she knew the answer.

It was as if it were being fired at her in an explosion from one of the cannons which stood along the sides of the deck.

She was in love!

In love with a man she had known for only a few days; a man who meant safety and security to her but who was in fact a pirate, an exile, a man with a price on his head, outlawed not only by the English but also by the French.

"I love him whatever he is!" Grania told her heart.

Because she could not bear to be away from him for one moment longer, she went to his side.

Chapter Six

Grania saw that St. Martin was not as beautiful as
Grenada with its mountains and its tropical vegetation,
but it was certainly very attractive with its golden
beaches.

She had also noticed many small, attractive bays as
they sailed alongside the island.

They dropped anchor, and although she realised that
it was not as secluded as Secret Harbour, it was nevertheless a good place for a pirate-ship to hide.

While the crew were busy furling the sails, the
Comte took Grania ashore and they walked a little way
up the low cliffs until in front of them she saw a very
attractive house.

It was quite small but resembled the older plantation
houses in Grenada and had the usual verandah over
which vines were growing profusely.

The *Comte* did not say anything and she wondered if
she should tell him how pretty she thought the house
looked, but she felt he was thinking of his real home in
Martinique and wishing they were there.

He opened the door with a key. Then as they walked
through a small Hall and into a Sitting-Room at one
side of it, she gave an exclamation of surprise.

The room was furnished with exquisite inlaid French
furniture, including some very fine marble-topped commodes with gilt handles and beautiful embellished feet.

On the walls were portraits which she knew without

being told were of the *Comte*'s ancestors, and she guessed these were the possessions he had brought to safety from his house in Martinique.

There were also many china ornaments, among which she recognised some pieces of Sèvres, while on the floor was a very fine Aubusson carpet.

"So this is where you hid your treasures!" she exclaimed.

"At least they should be safe here," he answered.

"I am so very, very glad you were able to bring them away."

She wanted to look at the paintings and the china, but the *Comte* said in a very different voice:

"I want to talk to you, Grania, so please listen to me."

She looked up at him enquiringly and he went on:

"You came to me for protection and that is what I want to give you. I am going now to find the woman who looks after this house in my absence and ask her if she will come here to sleep."

"But . . . why?" Grania asked. "And . . . where will . . . you be?"

"You must be aware that it would be quite wrong for me to stay here with you," the *Comte* replied. "I shall sleep in the ship with my crew and there will be nothing to frighten you."

Grania said nothing and after a moment he went on:

"I do not have to tell you that you must play your part of being a Frenchwoman at all times, and to do so you must speak French, think French, and to all intents and purposes *be* French."

"I will try," Grania said in a low voice, "but I thought now that we are here we could be . . . together."

She spoke pleadingly, but to her surprise the *Comte* was not looking at her but had turned his face away, and she had the feeling that he was going to say that was impossible.

Then at that moment there was a sudden shout from the front of the house, and the next minute they heard footsteps running across the verandah and Jean came bursting into the room.

"*Vite—vite! Monsieur!*" he said urgently. "*Un bateau en vue!*"

As he spoke he pointed in the direction of the sea.

"Stay here!" the *Comte* said abruptly to Grania.

Then he had gone from the house, closing the door behind him.

She went to the window to see him running towards the cliffs with Jean just ahead of him.

When he had gone, she stood looking out, and although she could see nothing she was frightened that there was danger, and she wished she were with the *Comte* and not left behind.

She knew that to see a ship at sea always spelt danger for him, and she had been well aware how all the way from Grenada the *Comte* had a look-out posted on the mast, and at the first indication that there was another ship in sight had immediately changed course.

She wondered if they had been seen coming into the bay, or if perhaps it was an English Man o' War intent on invading St. Martin.

The *Comte* and his friends had been quite certain that this would not happen, but there was always the chance that the English would change their minds and wish to add to their conquests amongst the islands.

It was all very perturbing, and although Grania stood for a long time at the window, hoping she would see some sign of their own ship or the one Jean had come to warn them about, there was only the blue horizon.

It grew more and more indistinct as the afternoon merged into evening and the sun began to sink.

She wanted to go to the top of the cliffs to see what was happening, but the *Comte* had told her to stay where she was, and because she loved him she wished to obey him.

After a little while she started to look round the small house, but it was hard to concentrate on anything but the fact that the *Comte* might be in danger, and she would not know what was happening.

Slowly she went upstairs and found one large, important bedroom, which she knew must be his, and several others.

They were all beautifully furnished, but the *Comte*'s bedroom had a magnificent French bed with curtains falling from a gold corola.

She knew he must have brought it here from Martinique, and she admired the painted dressing-table which was more suited to a woman than to a man.

There were small commodes on either side of the bed which she thought were the work of one of the great French craftsmen, and she realised that the paintings which were not of his ancestors were by Boucher.

It was all so lovely that she thought it was a room for love, then she blushed at her own thoughts.

She moved restlessly about until she went downstairs again to discover a small Dining-Room with more of the *Comte*'s ancestors on the walls and a kitchen which she was sure must delight Henri.

There was also a small room lined with books, and she told herself that at least here she would have plenty to read.

However, she had no wish to read at the moment. All she wanted was to be with the *Comte,* and again she went to the window, frightened because he had been away for so long.

Now the sun was sinking in a blaze of glory, and when the last crimson light disappeared, night came swiftly.

Although the stars were coming out one by one and a new moon was climbing up the sky, Grania thought she was encompassed by the darkness of despair and was afraid she would never see the *Comte* again.

Supposing he had sailed out to sea to investigate the enemy ship, and there had been a battle? Supposing he had been defeated and was either drowned or taken prisoner?

She did not know what would happen to her if she was never to see him again.

She wanted to cry out at the agony of knowing he had disappeared and there would be no-one to help her.

What was more, she knew despairingly, since her luggage had not been brought ashore, that she had no money and no possessions. But that was immaterial beside the fact that she had lost the *Comte*.

Now she thought her agony was like a thousand knives piercing her heart and making her suffer in a way that was almost unbearable.

Because her eyes ached from staring into the darkness, she moved across the room, feeling her way to a chair, and sat down.

She put her head in her hands, half-praying, half just suffering helplessly like a small animal caught in a trap.

"Send him back to me ... please, God, send him ... back to me," she prayed.

She felt as if the darkness suffocated her and she was completely and utterly lost!

Suddenly when she felt she could bear it no longer and must go to the bay and look for him, the front door opened and he was there.

She could not see him, but she gave a little cry that seemed to echo round the walls and ran instinctively to find him.

She threw herself against him, put her arms round his neck, holding on to him and crying as she did so:

"You ... have come ... back! I thought I had ... lost you! I was frightened ... so desperately ... frightened that I would ... never see you ... again!"

The words fell over themselves, and because she had been so frightened and her relief at his return was so overwhelming, she cried involuntarily:

"I love you ... and I cannot ... live without ... you!"

The *Comte* threw something he was carrying down on the floor and put his arms round her.

He held her so tightly that she could hardly breathe, then his lips came down on hers.

As she felt his mouth hold her captive she knew that this was what she had been wanting, what she had been yearning for, and what she had thought she would never know.

His kiss was fierce, demanding, insistent, and she felt as if she gave him her heart, her soul, her whole self.

The agony of fear she had been feeling was gone. Instead there was an indescribable rapture, an ecstasy that seemed to fill the room with a light which came from within themselves.

The wonder of it told her that this was not just human love but something more perfect and part of the Divine.

When the *Comte* had kissed her until she felt that she was no longer herself but utterly and completely his, he raised his head to say in a voice that was unsteady:

"My darling, I did not mean this to happen."

"I love . . . you!"

"And I love you," he answered. "I fought against it and tried to prevent myself from saying so, but you have made it impossible."

"I . . . thought I had . . . lost you."

"You will never do that as long as I am alive," he replied, "but, *ma cherie*, I have been trying to protect you from myself and from my love."

"You . . . love me?"

"Of course I love you!" he said almost angrily. "But it is something I should not do any more than that you should love me."

"How can I help it?" Grania asked.

Then he was kissing her again, kissing her until she felt as if he carried her into the sky and there were no problems, no difficulties, nothing but themselves and their love.

*   *   *

A long time later the *Comte* said:

"Let me light the candles, my precious. We can

hardly stay here in the dark forever, although I want to go on kissing you."

"That is . . . what I want . . . you to . . . do," Grania said breathlessly.

He kissed her again. Then with an effort he took his arms from her and walked a few steps to a table at the side of the stairs.

He lit a candle and Grania could see him. She thought his face in the light was illuminated as if by some celestial fire.

His eyes were on her, but as if he forced himself not to take her in his arms he lit a taper from the candle and went into the Sitting-Room to light the candles there.

Only when the room was illuminated and looking very beautiful did he say:

"Forgive me for upsetting you, *ma petite*."

"What happened? What was the . . . boat you went to . . . investigate? Was it . . . English?"

The *Comte* blew out the taper.

Then he walked towards Grania and put his arms round her again.

"I know what you have been thinking," he said. "It was an English boat which my crew had sighted, but it constituted no danger to us."

Grania gave a cry of relief and put her head against his shoulder. The *Comte* kissed her forehead before he went on:

"But in a way it may concern you."

"Concern me?" Grania asked in surprise.

"There must have been a battle not far from here," he said, "perhaps two or three days ago."

It was difficult for Grania to listen because she was so content to be in his arms.

'He is with me and I am safe,' she kept thinking to herself.

"I imagine," the *Comte* went on, "that the English Man o' War H.M.S. *Heroic* was sunk, because the boat which Jean came to tell us about was from that ship. It contained an Officer and eight ratings."

"They were . . . English?" Grania asked nervously.

"They were English," the *Comte* replied, "but they were all dead!"

It seemed wrong, Grania knew, but she could not help feeling relieved that they could therefore constitute no danger to the *Comte* and his crew.

"There was nothing we could do for them," the *Comte* continued, "except bury them at sea, but I took their papers, which will prove their identity should it ever be necessary."

He paused before he added:

"The Officer's name, and he was a Commander, was Patrick O'Kerry."

Grania stiffened.

"Patrick O'Kerry?" she repeated.

"I thought he might be some relation of your, and I have brought you his papers and also his jacket and cap in case you would wish to keep them."

There was a little pause. Then Grania said:

"Patrick was . . . my cousin . . . and although I hardly knew him . . . Papa will be very upset."

"We will have to let him know sometime."

"Yes . . . of course," Grania agreed, "and he will be upset because Patrick was not only his . . . nephew, he was also . . . his heir . . . and now there are . . . no more O'Kerrys and the . . . title will die out."

"I can understand how that would upset your father."

"There is certainly not much to inherit," Grania said, "but Papa was the fourth Earl, and now there will never be a fifth."

"I am sorry about that," the *Comte* said softly. "I did not want to upset you, my darling."

Because his arms were round her again and his lips were on her cheek, it was hard for Grania to feel anything but the joy that he was touching her.

At the same time, it seemed such a waste of life.

Her cousin Patrick, who had called to see her mother when they were in London, had been so excited at being posted to a new ship and going out to the

Caribbean. It seemed tragic now to think that he was dead.

She remembered how he had talked to her mother about the West Indies, and Grania had thought him a pleasant young man, but he had not paid her much attention as she was only a School-girl.

"What I think is very surprising," the *Comte* said, "is that your cousin was dark. Somehow I expected that all your relations would be fair like you."

Grania gave him a faint little smile.

"There are fair O'Kerrys like Papa and me, and there are also dark ones who are supposed to have Spanish blood in them."

She thought the *Comte* was surprised, and she explained:

"When the ships of the Spanish Armada on their way to invade England were wrecked on the south coast of Ireland, many of the Spanish sailors never returned home."

The *Comte* smiled.

"So they found the O'Kerry ladies attractive."

"I suppose they must have done so," Grania replied, "and they certainly left their imprint on the future generations."

"No wonder some are dark and some are fair," the *Comte* said, "but I prefer you fair, and one day, *ma belle*, you can revert to looking English. But I am afraid that whatever the colour of your hair, you will be French."

Grania looked up at him questioningly and he said:

"You will marry me? I thought I could pretend you were my cousin and keep you at arm's-length, but you have made it impossible."

"I do not . . . wish to be at . . . arm's-length," Grania murmured, "and I want . . . to be your . . . wife."

"Heaven knows what sort of life I can offer you," the *Comte* said, "and you know I have nothing to give you but my heart."

"I do not want anything else," Grania answered. "But

are you quite ... quite sure I shall not be an ...
encumbrance and you will ... not regret marrying
me?"

"That would be impossible," the *Comte* said. "I have
been looking for you all my life, and now that I have
found you, whatever is the right and proper or sensible
thing to do, I know I cannot lose you."

Then he was kissing her again, and it was impossible
to think but only to feel.

* * *

A long time later the *Comte* said with a sigh:

"As soon as Henri arrives to prepare our dinner, I will
go to see the Priest and arrange that we shall be
married first thing tomorrow morning."

He kissed her before he asked:

"You will not mind a Catholic wedding, my darling?
It would look very strange if my bride belonged to
another Church."

"As long as we are married, I do not care what sort
of Church it takes place in, but as it happens I was
baptised a Catholic."

The *Comte* looked at her incredulously.

"Do you mean that?"

Grania nodded.

"Papa was Catholic but Mama was not. They were
married in a Catholic Church and I was baptised in
one."

The *Comte* was still looking astonished, and she went
on:

"I am afraid Papa was not a very good Catholic even
when we lived in England, and when we came to
Grenada he realised that the British were very much
against Catholicism because of their anti-French feelings and so he did not attend any Church."

She thought the *Comte* was shocked, and she went
on quickly:

"When Mama was in St. George's she attended the
Protestant Church and sometimes she took me with her
on Sundays, but it was a very long way to go, and

because it upset Papa when we left him alone it did not
happen very often."

The *Comte* held her close to him.

"When you marry me, my precious," he said, "you
will become a good Catholic, and together we will
thank God that He has enabled us to find each other. I
have a feeling that from now on He will protect us both
and keep us safe."

"I feel that too," Grania said, "and you know I will
do . . . anything . . . anything you ask me to."

The way she spoke made the *Comte* kiss her again,
and they only drew apart when they heard Henri come
into the kitchen and knew he was preparing the dinner.

When the *Comte* left to visit the Priest, Jean arrived
with one of Grania's trunks and she started to change
her clothes.

She had a bath, which was very cooling after the heat
of the day, and although she protested to Jean that she
should not be taking the *Comte*'s bedroom from him,
he told her that those were his Master's orders and
after that she did not argue.

She only remembered as she undressed that tomorrow they would be together, and she knew that God
had not only saved her from marrying Roderick Maigrin
but had given her the man of her dreams.

"How can I be so lucky?" she asked herself.

Then fervently she was saying Catholic prayers which
she knew were the ones that the *Comte* said and which
would be hers in the future.

When he returned she heard him go to another room
where Jean had laid out his evening-clothes.

By this time Grania had found a pretty gown into
which she could change, and she arranged her hair in
the smartest fashion she knew.

She could not help wishing that it were fair again,
but she knew that nothing mattered as long as the
Comte loved her and that she must remember what he
had said to her—to think French and to be French, so
that nobody would suspect for a moment that she was an
enemy.

"Once I am the *Comtesse* de Vence there will be no need for pretence," she said to her reflection in the mirror, "for then I shall have the most beautiful title in the world."

She was still looking in the mirror but was thinking of the *Comte* when there was a knock on the door and he came into the room.

"I thought you would be ready, my precious."

Then as she rose from the stool in front of the dressing-table he held out his arms and she ran towards him.

He did not kiss her, but there was an expression of infinite tenderness in his eyes.

"It is all arranged," he said. "Tomorrow you will become my wife. We will sleep together in the bed which belonged to my grandfather and was so much a part of my home that I could not leave it behind."

"I thought that was what it must be."

He came a little closer and Grania asked:

"Are you really going to marry me?"

"You will be my wife and we will face all the problems and difficulties together."

He looked round the room as he said:

"I was thinking as I was coming back from the Church that at least for a little while we will not starve."

His eyes rested on the Boucher painting as he spoke, and Grania gave a cry.

"You do not mean that you intend to sell that painting?"

"I shall get a good price for it from the Dutch on the other side of the island," the *Comte* replied. "Being neutral, they have gained from the war rather than lost."

"But you cannot sell your family treasures!"

"I have the only treasure which really matters to me now," he answered.

His lips swept away any further protest that she might have made.

They went downstairs hand-in-hand, and Jean served them the delicious dinner that Henri had cooked, and when it was finished and they were alone the *Comte* said:

"I have arranged for the Housekeeper who looks after the Priest's house to sleep here tonight so that you will be chaperoned. I would not want us to start our married life by shocking the French matrons of St. Martin, whose tongues wag like those of women in every part of the world."

"You will sleep in the ship?"

"In the bed in which you slept last night," the *Comte* replied. "I will dream of you, and tomorrow my dreams will come true."

"And I shall be dreaming too."

"I love you!" he said. "I love you so much that every moment I think I have reached my fullest capability of love, and then suddenly I love you infinitely more! What have you done to me, my darling, that I should feel like a boy in love for the first time?"

"But you must have loved so many women," Grania murmured.

The *Comte* smiled.

"I am French. I find women very attractive, but unlike most of my countrymen I resisted having an arranged marriage when I was young, and I have never, and this is the truth, found a woman until now with whom I would wish to share the rest of my life."

"Suppose I disappoint you?"

"You will never do that. I knew when I looked at what I thought was your portrait that you were everything I wanted in a woman, and when I actually saw you I knew that I had underestimated both my need and what you can give me."

"You are . . . sure of that?" Grania enquired.

"Absolutely sure," he replied. "It is not so much what you say or even what you think, my precious, but what you are. Your sweetness, which I recognised the first time I set my eyes on you, shines like a beacon and envelops you with an aura of purity and goodness that could only come from God."

Grania clasped her hands together.

"You say such wonderful things to me! I am only so desperately afraid that I will not be able to live up to what you expect of me, and then perhaps you will sail away and leave me."

The *Comte* shook his head.

"You must know that I have now ceased to be a pirate. After we are married I will talk to my friends and we will think out some other ways that we can all make a living."

He thought before he went on:

"As I have said, I will sell some of my possessions so that we will not starve, and because I know God will not fail us, perhaps it will not be long before we can return to Martinique."

The way he spoke seemed somehow inspired, so that the tears came into Grania's eyes and she put out her hands towards his.

"I shall pray and pray," she said, "and, darling, you must teach me to be good, so that my prayers are heard."

"I know that you need no teaching in that respect," the *Comte* replied, "but there are many other things that I intend to teach you, my adorable one, and I think you can guess what those lessons are."

Grania blushed. Then she said:

"I only hope you will not be . . . dissatisfied with your . . . pupil."

The *Comte* left the table and drawing Grania to her feet put his arm round her, and they moved into the Sitting-Room.

It looked so lovely in the candle-light that Grania thought they might be in a *Château* in France or in one of the Palaces that she had read about in the books which her mother had bought to make her more proficient in the French language.

She wanted to say that she could not bear any of the things in the room to be sold, but she knew it would be a mistake to upset the *Comte* and make him realise even more fully than he did already the sacrifices he had to make.

'At least I have some money,' Grania thought.

She knew that her English sovereigns when changed into French francs would amount to quite a considerable sum of money.

She smiled because she was glad she could contribute to their life together, and the *Comte* asked:

"What has made you smile, except happiness, *ma petite?*"

"I was thinking I am so glad that I have some money with me. Tomorrow it will be yours legally, but before you tell me you are too proud to take it, I suggest it could contribute to what you have to spend on your friends and the other members of the crew. After all, it is my fault that they can no longer continue to be pirates."

The *Comte* put his cheek against hers.

"I adore you, my lovely one," he said, "and I am not going to argue because, as you said, it is your fault that we shall have to settle down and behave like respectable Frenchmen. But before we sell the ship, which will undoubtedly fetch a very good price, we must sail back to Grenada to tell your father of the death of your cousin, and also to see that he himself is safe."

"Can we do that?" Grania asked. "I am worried about Papa, especially when he is with Mr. Maigrin."

"We will go together because it is the right thing to do. I also think your father should know that his daughter is married, although perhaps he will not be very pleased that it is to a Frenchman."

Grania gave a little laugh.

"My father will not mind that. You must remember he is Irish, and the Irish have never liked the English."

The *Comte* laughed too.

"I had forgotten that! So if your father will tolerate me as a son-in-law, perhaps when things are better than they are at the moment he will be able to come and stay with us in St. Martin and you will be able to go and stay in Grenada."

"It is kind of you to think like that," Grania said,

"because I feel in a way I ought to look after Papa."

As she spoke she knew that it was only a day-dream, for as long as her father persisted in his friendship with Roderick Maigrin it was impossible for them to be together.

She was quite certain that if Maigrin learnt that she was married to a Frenchman he would try to destroy the *Comte* either by shooting him as an enemy or by having him pursued and persecuted by the English.

Yet she must have news of her father, and perhaps if he was still at Maigrin House she would, on some pretext or other, be able to inveigle him to Secret Harbour.

There she could at least say good-bye to him before she returned to live at St. Martin.

Then it flashed through her mind how fine the *Comte* was once again to anticipate her wishes almost before she had thought of them herself.

Because she wanted so desperately to kiss him, she could only move closer into his arms and feel his lips seeking hers.

* * *

Grania was awake very early because she was so excited and also because she heard movements downstairs and knew that Jean and Henri were already up and about.

Then she thought of the room next door where the Priest's Housekeeper, an elderly woman with a kind face, was sleeping.

She had arrived last night carrying a lantern to light her way through the rough land which lay just behind the house.

"I am delighted to meet you, *M'mselle*," she had said to Grania. "Father François sends you his blessing and is looking forward to marrying you to *Monsieur le Comte* at nine-thirty tomorrow morning."

"*Merci, Madame*," Grania replied, "and thank you too for coming here tonight to keep me company. It was very kind of you."

"We all have to do what we can for those who have been stricken by the cruelties of war."

The *Comte* said good-night, as the Housekeeper was there, and kissed Grania's hands before he returned to the ship.

When he had gone, the Housekeeper said:

"That's a fine man and a very good Catholic, *M'mselle*. You're very fortunate to have such a man for your husband."

"Very fortunate indeed, *Madame*," Grania agreed, "and I am very grateful."

"I shall pray for you both," the Housekeeper said, "and I know *le bon Dieu* will give you great happiness."

Grania was certain that was true, and she lay awake in the beautiful bed with its gold corola, thinking how wonderfully lucky she was and feeling that her mother knew of her happiness.

"How could I have known . . . how could I have guessed that I would be . . . saved at the . . . last moment from that terrible Mr. Maigrin?" Grania asked herself.

Then once again she was praying disjointed prayers of gratitude, disjointed because even to pray about the *Comte* made her feel again the rapture and the ecstasy he evoked in her when he kissed her and made her aware of strange feelings that were different from anything she had ever known before.

Then finally when she fell asleep it was to feel that God was watching over her and making tomorrow come quickly.

* * *

As the sunshine filled the room Grania thought it was an omen of what her life would be like in the future.

Outside, birds were singing, the vivid colours of the bougainvillaea in the garden vied with those of the vines climbing over the verandah, and the emerald of the sea against the horizon all seemed part of a dream.

"But it is true . . . really true!" Grania cried, and knew this was her wedding-day.

She did not have a wedding-dress, but amongst the things her mother had bought for her there was a gown specially to wear when she was presented at Court.

It was white, which was correct for a Débutante, and it had been delivered after her mother had died.

Grania had in fact debated whether she should try to sell it back to the dressmaker because she felt she would never have a use for it.

Then she had thought it would be humiliating to say that she not only would be unable to wear it but could not really afford to pay for it. So she reluctantly handed over the money and had brought it out with her to Grenada.

As she drew it out from the trunk she knew that while it was a trifle over-elaborate, it would be suitable for a bride and perhaps would make her look beautiful for the *Comte*.

She had no veil, and when she explained this to the Housekeeper, who had come into her room to help her dress, the woman sent Jean hastily to the Priest's house.

"We have a veil which we sometimes lend to young brides," she said, "if they arrive at the Church with only a wreath on their heads, because Father François does not consider that respectful enough in the House of God."

"I should be very happy if I could borrow it," Grania replied.

"It will be a pleasure!" the Housekeeper said. "And I will make you a wreath which will be far prettier than anything you could buy."

She sent Henri hurrying into the garden and when he came back with a basket full of white flowers, she sat in Grania's bedroom arranging them skilfully in the form of a wreath.

When she had finished, nothing could have been prettier than the fresh white flowers with their green leaves, which were more becoming than any artificial wreath could ever have been.

The veil was of very fine lace and fell over Grania's shoulders, giving her an ethereal appearance, and when the wreath was arranged over it the Housekeeper stood back to survey her work and said in awe-struck tones:

"You make a very beautiful bride, *M'mselle*. No man could fail to appreciate such a lovely wife."

"I hope you are right," Grania said simply.

When she went downstairs to the Sitting-Room where the *Comte* was waiting, she knew by the expression on his face that she was everything he had expected, and more.

He looked at her for a long moment before he said very quietly:

"I did not believe anyone could be so beautiful."

She smiled at him through her veil.

"I love you!"

"I will be able to tell you later how much I love you," he answered, "but now I dare not touch you. I only want to go down on my knees and light candles to you, for I not only love you but worship you."

"You must not . . . say such things," Grania protested. "It makes me . . . afraid that I am not . . . good enough."

He smiled as if she was being absurd. Then he kissed her hand before he said:

"Our carriage is waiting at the back of the house. Because the crew did not think the horses pulling it were fine enough, they themselves are going to draw us to the Church."

Grania gave an exclamation of surprise, and when she walked outside she saw that the light open carriage was horseless while the shafts were ready to be pulled by all the young members of the crew.

The carriage itself had been decorated with the same white flowers that had made her wreath, and there was also a bouquet of them on the seat.

As they moved away, Grania thought that it was just the sort of fairy-tale wedding that she wanted to have.

The *Comte* held her hand tightly in his as they were pulled down a narrow road which led to the small village.

It consisted of only a few West Indian "ginger-bread" houses with wrought-iron balconies.

They were built on the edge of the sea and inland

behind them Grania could see several steep hills forming
a very lovely view.

The small ancient Church was full, and as the Priest
met them at the door and led them inside, the *Comte*'s
friends and all those who had not been pulling the
carriage were waiting to watch the marriage take place.

To Grania it was a very moving service and she felt as
if the fragrant incense rising towards the roof carried
their prayers up to God and that He Himself blessed
them and their love for each other.

She was very conscious of the wedding-ring on her
finger, but more than anything else of the *Comte* kneel-
ing beside her and his voice repeating his vows with an
unmistakable sincerity.

Last night she had said to him a little nervously:

"If I am to be . . . married as your . . . cousin, will it
be . . . legal?"

"I thought you might ask that question," he said. "As
you know, we shall only be called by our Christian
names, and therefore I have already told the Priest that
you were Christened 'Teresa Grania.'"

"I thought I was to be 'Gabrielle'?"

"I thought 'Gabrielle Grania' sounded too much of a
mouthful," the *Comte* replied, and they both laughed.

"'Teresa' is a very pretty name, and I am quite
content with it," Grania said.

She found out at the Service that her husband had
other names, when as he repeated his vows he said:

"I, Beaufort Francis Louis . . ."

When they left the little Church and were drawn
back in their carriage to their own house, Grania could
think of nothing except the man beside her and the
words of love that he whispered in her ear.

Then they were joined by everyone who had watched
the ceremony, and some friends too who lived on the
island. There was wine with which to drink their health
and food which Grania was sure Henri must have spent
most of the night preparing.

It was all very happy and gay, with a laughter that
seemed part of the sunshine.

Then at last somewhat reluctantly the people began to leave.

First the friends who lived on the island, then the Priest and his Housekeeper, and finally when it was time for *siesta* the crew said they must go back to the ship.

It was then that Grania realised that she was alone with her husband, and she turned to look at him, raising her face to his.

"I think," he said, "we would both be more comfortable if we had our *siesta* without being encumbered by our smart clothes, and I am very much afraid of spoiling that beautiful gown."

"It was meant to be worn at Buckingham Palace," Grania replied, "but it is much, much more appropriate that I should wear it on the day I was married to you."

"I agree with you," the *Comte* said with a smile. "Why should we worry about Kings and Queens when we have each other?"

He drew her up the stairs and when they reached the bedroom Grania realised that somebody—she expected it was Jean—had lowered the sun-blinds so that the room was cool and dim.

It was fragrant with flowers which Jean must have arranged for when they came back from the Church, and they stood in great vases on the dressing-table and on either side of the bed.

"My bride!" the *Comte* said very softly.

Then he took the wreath from her head and lifted her veil.

He looked at her for a long moment before he took her in his arms.

"You are real!" he said almost as if he spoke to himself. "When I was marrying you I was half-afraid that you were a goddess who had come down from the top of one of the mountains or a nymph from a cascade."

"I am . . . real," Grania whispered, "but like you I feel that this is all a dream."

"If it is," the *Comte* said, "then let us go on dreaming!"

Chapter Seven

Grania awoke and felt that her heart was singing like the birds outside the window, and she looked adoringly towards the *Comte* sleeping beside her.

She knew that every day and every night she spent with him she loved him more.

But today was special because they were leaving for Grenada.

They had been married for over three weeks and yesterday the *Comte* had said:

"I think, my darling, we must take our last trip in the ship before I sell it."

Grania looked at him in a startled manner and he had explained:

"I intend to sell the ship first. That will give all the crew and myself enough money for us to look round and plan our futures. After that, if no-one is settled, other things will have to go."

The way he spoke of "other things" told Grania how much he minded the thought of having to part with his paintings and treasures, which she had learnt had been collected by his ancestors over many centuries.

"They were so fortunate that they were able to bring them away from France before the Revolution," he had said. "Otherwise everything we owned would either have been confiscated or burnt by the peasants."

There was a little silence and Grania knew that he

was thinking that he would like to keep them intact for his eldest son, but that would not be possible.

She moved away from him to say after a moment:

"Sometimes I feel I should have left you . . . roaming the sea as a . . . pirate."

The *Comte* laughed and it swept the expression of regret from his eyes.

"My darling, do you think I would really want to be a pirate if it meant I had to leave you? I am so happy that I thank God every day that we are together and you are my wife. At the same time, we have to live."

"Yes, I know that," Grania said, "but . . ."

To keep her from apologising any further, he kissed her, and the rapture and wonder of it took everything else out of her mind.

Now knowing that the ship was for sale, she prayed that it would fetch enough money for it to be a very, very long time before the *Comte* had to sell anything else.

She knew also that he was right in saying that before they were marooned on St. Martin with no means of getting away she must find out how her father was and, if possible, tell him of her marriage.

Because it meant leaving even for a little while the *Comte*'s small house and the happiness she had found there, she pressed herself against him.

He awoke and without opening his eyes he put his arms round her to hold her close, and she said:

"We will not take any risks, will we? If it is not safe to go ashore at Grenada, you will turn back?"

The *Comte* looked at her.

"You do not think, my adorable, wonderful little wife, that I would take you anywhere where there was danger? I promise that if Abe's white flag does not tell us everything is safe we will turn back immediately."

"That is all I want to know," Grania said. "If anything should happen to you now, I would want . . . to die!"

"Do not talk of dying," he answered. "You are going to live, and we will see our children and our grandchildren running the plantations at Martinique before we either of us leave each other or this earth."

He spoke prophetically and Grania put her arm round his neck to draw his lips close to hers.

"How can I tell you how much I love you?" she asked.

"Like this!"

Then he was kissing her, his heart was beating against hers, and as she felt the fire rising in him she knew the flames he evoked were rising in her too.

Then it seemed to Grania that there was the music of the angels and a celestial light which covered them like the blessing of God, and they were one. . . .

* * *

The sea was vividly blue and emerald, the sky was dazzling with the sunshine, and as the sails billowed out in the breeze the ship seemed to be skimming over the smooth water rather than sailing through it.

The crew were whistling and singing as they worked, and Grania had the feeling that like the *Comte* they were content to give up the risky, dangerous life of piracy and return to what he called "respectability."

Every night over dinner they talked of what they could do.

"It is a pity there are not more people on St. Martin and that there is no crime," Leo said, "otherwise they would need my services."

"No crime?" Grania questioned.

He shook his head.

"If anybody stole, how could they get away with the spoils? And everyone is so good-natured that nobody wants to murder anyone."

"It seems a waste of your intelligence," the *Comte* said, "but when we get home I am sure there will be hundreds of cases waiting for you to deal with them."

They always talked optimistically of the time when they would return to Martinique, and the clerks who had worked in Leo's office were, Grania knew, studying in the evenings so that they would not be behind in preparation for their Examinations, however long they had to wait before they took them.

She had by now a real affection for the three men who were so close to her husband, and she also found that the rest of the crew not only admired her but sought her help with their problems and wanted to talk to her about their futures.

"I am sure every woman in the world would envy me if they knew I had so many delightful men all to myself," Grania said to the *Comte*.

"You belong to me, *ma petite*, and if I find you so much as looking at another man, you will find I am very jealous!"

She pressed herself nearer to him as she said:

"You know I could never look at anybody but you. I love you so much that sometimes I am afraid you will be bored with my telling you so and go in search of somebody less predictable."

"I want your love," he said, "and you do not love me yet half as much as I intend you to do."

He had then kissed her fiercely and demandingly as if he would force her to realise how much he needed her.

As they saw no ships on the voyage towards Grenada it took them less time than it had taken when they had left it for St. Martin.

The afternoon before they reached the island Henri came to the cabin after the *siesta* to help Grania wash the rinse out of her hair.

She had to apply it again every time it was washed, but this time it had to be washed out thoroughly so that when she landed on Grenada she looked English.

She dried her hair in the sunshine and when it was dry she left it hanging over her shoulders.

The *Comte* had been busy on deck steering the ship, and when he came into the cabin as the sun was sinking he saw Grania standing by a porthole and for a moment he stood still, looking at her.

Then he smiled and said:

"I see I have an English visitor! I am delighted to meet you, Mrs. Vence!"

Grania laughed and ran towards him.

"That is perfect!" she said. "Now you speak English far better than I speak French."

"That would be impossible," the *Comte* replied, "but I am glad your lessons are having an effect."

"You speak just like an Englishman," she said, "but I feel that you look almost too smart to be one."

"You flatter me," the *Comte* answered. "But, darling, whatever you may look like, remember that you are my wife, my very fascinating, alluring French wife."

He kissed her. Then he drew up her hair across her face and kissed her through it.

"You are my golden girl again," he said. "I am not certain how I like you best, dark and mysterious like the dusk, or shining and golden as a spring morning."

The *Comte* had planned that they should draw near Grenada well after sunrise—not too early in case Abe did not have time to change the flag. But they were slowed down by lack of wind, and when they finally arrived within sight of the island it was about eleven o'clock.

Grania was on the poop-deck beside the *Comte* and they were both waiting for the signal from the look-out on the mast.

He held a telescope to his eye and nobody on deck spoke until finally they heard him cry:

"A white flag! I can see it quite clearly!"

The *Comte* swung the wheel over, the sails filled with the breeze, and they shot ahead.

It was quite a feat to enter the bay of Secret Harbour, but the *Comte* managed it brilliantly and Grania felt a little tug at her heart when she saw the jetty, the pine trees, and the brilliant bushes of bougainvillaea that she had known ever since she was a child.

They let down the anchor, the gang-plank joined the deck to the jetty, and the *Comte* helped Grania onto it.

They had arranged to go ahead while the others

stayed on the ship, ready to move away quickly if it was necessary.

"If Papa is here I want him to meet everybody," Grania said.

"We will have to see what your father thinks of me first," the *Comte* replied. "He may disapprove violently of your marrying a Frenchman."

"No-one could disapprove of you," Grania answered, and the *Comte* laughed and kissed the tip of her nose.

Now he was carrying over his arm Patrick O'Kerry's uniform coat, and the papers he had taken from him before he was buried at sea were in the pocket.

"Papa will want to keep them," Grania said, "and one day when the war is over, if she is still alive I am sure his mother would wish to have them."

"That is what I thought," the *Comte* answered.

"How can you be so kind?" Grania asked. "I cannot believe that any other man would think of such things in the middle of a war."

"A war which I pray will not concern us in the future," the *Comte* said beneath his breath.

Because she was so closely attuned to him Grania was aware that he was in fact apprehensive as to what sort of reception he would receive from his father-in-law.

But she was confident that unless Roderick Maigrin was with her father, he would be glad that she had found somebody to love and who loved her.

If her father was not at Secret Harbour she was wondering how she could manage to send for him so that he came alone.

It was not possible to predict exactly what would happen when they arrived, but what was important was that she should first see Abe and find out what the position was.

They walked through the pine trees and she glanced at the *Comte* before they left their shelter for the garden.

She knew he was looking serious but, she thought, exceedingly handsome.

Because it was so hot he was wearing only a thin

linen shirt, but his cravat was tied in an intricate fashion which always fascinated her, and his white cotton breeches were the same as the crew wore, only better-fitting.

'He is so smart,' Grania thought to herself, 'but at the same time so masculine.'

She blushed at her own thoughts.

They walked through the overgrown flower-beds which had been her mother's pride.

Then, just as they reached the centre of the garden and the house lay straight ahead of them, a man appeared on the verandah.

One glance at him and Grania felt her heart stand still, for he was wearing a British uniform and was, she saw, a Colonel.

Both she and the *Comte* stopped and neither of them moved as the Colonel came down the steps and walked towards them.

Then behind him Grania saw Abe and knew by the expression of consternation on his face that the English Officer's visit was unexpected.

The Colonel came forward. Then as he reached them he held out his hand to Grania and smiled.

"I think you must be Lady Grania O'Kerry," he said. "May I introduce myself? I am Lieutenant-Colonel Campbell and I have just arrived from Barbados with a transport of troops."

For a moment Grania thought it was impossible to speak.

Then she said in a voice that did not sound like her own:

"How do you do, Colonel? I am sure you were very welcome at St. George's."

"We were," the Colonel replied, "and I think we can soon get the trouble here cleared up."

He glanced at the *Comte* and Grania knew he was waiting to be introduced.

Then as she wondered frantically what she should say, she saw the Colonel's eyes resting on the Naval Officer's coat that the *Comte* carried on his arm.

Almost like a message from Heaven, Grania knew what she could do.

"May I, Colonel, introduce my cousin, who is also my husband? Commander Patrick O'Kerry!"

The *Comte* and the Colonel shook hands and the Colonel said:

"I am delighted to meet you, Commander. Strangely enough, the Governor was speaking about you today and wondering how he could get in touch with you."

"What about?" the *Comte* asked.

Grania thought he sounded completely composed, while her heart was beating frantically.

The Colonel turned again to her.

"I am afraid, Lady Grania," he said quietly, "I am the bearer of bad news."

"Bad . . . news?" Grania repeated almost beneath her breath.

"I am here to inform you that your father, the Earl of Kilkerry, was killed by the revolutionaries."

Grania drew in her breath and put out her hand towards the *Comte*.

He took it in his and she felt as if the clasp of his fingers gave her strength.

"What . . . happened?"

"Ten days ago the slaves on Mr. Roderick Maigrin's plantation were determined to join the other rebels," the Colonel replied. "However, he became aware of it and tried to prevent them from leaving."

Grania was sure that he had killed them as he had killed the others, but she did not say anything, and the Colonel went on:

"However, they disarmed him and shot your father, who died instantly. But they tortured Mr. Maigrin before they finally murdered him."

Grania did not speak. She could only feel relief that her father had died without suffering.

Then the *Comte* spoke.

"You will understand, Colonel, that this has been a great shock for my wife. May I suggest that we go into the house so that she can sit down?"

"Yes, of course," the Colonel agreed.

The *Comte's* arm went round Grania and as they walked across the garden and up the stairs she realised that he was limping most convincingly.

She wondered vaguely why he was doing so.

When they were seated in her mother's Drawing-Room and Abe without being asked had brought them rum punches, the Colonel said:

"I suppose, Commander, you are anxious to get back to sea?"

"I am afraid that will be impossible for some time," the *Comte* replied. "As you are doubtless aware, I was on H.M.S. *Heroic,* which was sunk, and I, with a number of other men, was wounded."

"I noticed you limped," the Colonel said, "but apart from your wound, as your circumstances have now changed, I am hoping we can perhaps persuade you to stay here."

The *Comte* looked surprised and the Colonel explained:

"As I think you must be aware, you are now the Earl of Kilkerry, and the reason that the bodies of the murdered gentlemen were discovered was that the Governor was anxious that the plantations should be put back into order and the slaves set to work."

Grania raised her head to say:

"I think . . . perhaps we have . . . very few slaves . . . left."

"I expect that is true, as it is on most of the plantations where many of the slaves have run away to join the rebels, and the rest are hiding. But we shall soon take Belvedere, and once Fédor is in our hands the rebellion will be over."

"So the slaves will go back to work and will be anxious to do so," the *Comte* remarked.

"Exactly!" the Colonel agreed. "And that is why, My Lord, I would like you to stay here and run the estate for your wife. It is important to the island, and perhaps until we can find somebody to take over Mr. Maigrin's plantation you might have time to keep an eye on his land as well as your own."

There was a moment's pause while Grania knew that the *Comte* was thinking. Then he said:

"I will certainly do the best I can for you, and I am certain I can see that our own slaves are content and forget any rebellious feelings they may have had."

The Colonel smiled.

"That is exactly what I want to hear, My Lord, and I am sure the Governor will be delighted by your attitude."

He paused before he added:

"By the way, Lady Grania, I know you will be sorry to hear that the old Governor, whom you knew well, was killed by the rebels, and the present Governor is new to the island. He will, I know, be happy to make your acquaintance later. I need not add that at the moment he is far too busy for any social engagements."

"Yes, of course," Grania said. "We will be busy too. I am afraid my father has rather neglected the plantation in the last two or three years and there is a great deal to be done."

"I am quite sure your husband will manage admirably."

The Colonel finished his rum punch and rose to his feet.

"Now, if you will forgive me," he said, "I must be on my way. I have to get back to St. George's. The Governor asked me as I was clearing up certain difficulties in St. David's to call here on my way home, and I was exceedingly fortunate to find you."

"We shall hope to see you again," Grania said, holding out her hand.

"I shall hope so too," the Colonel replied. "But as soon as our plans are clarified we will go into action!"

He shook hands with the *Comte*, saying:

"Good-bye, My Lord. The very best of luck! May I say I am delighted that you are here. You may not know it, but there were very few survivors from H.M.S. *Heroic*."

The *Comte* saw the Colonel to the door where his

horse was waiting and a dozen or so troops were mounted.

He watched them ride away, then went back to the Drawing-Room.

As he came through the door Grania ran towards him to fling her arms round him.

"Darling, you were wonderful!" she said. "He had not the least suspicion that you were not who you said you were."

"Who *you* said I was," the *Comte* corrected, "and I thought it was very quick and clever of you."

He drew her to the sofa and sat down beside her, holding her hand in his.

She looked up at him enquiringly and he said very quietly:

"This is a decision which you and only you can make. Are we to stay or are we to leave?"

Grania did not pause before she asked:

"Would you be willing to stay here and run the plantation as the Colonel suggested?"

"Why not? It belongs to you, and I am quite certain it will be hard work, but with the experience I have we could make it pay."

He did not wait for Grania to say anything but went on:

"If we are here we can also find work for all our friends, and your job, my darling, will be to make them proficient not on a plantation but in the English language."

He smiled as he went on:

"After all, they are all intelligent Frenchmen, and it should not be hard for Leo eventually to find plenty of work in St. George's, and if we are clever André and Jacques can take over Roderick Maigrin's plantation."

Grania gave a little cry.

"That would be wonderful, and in a way poetic justice after that man was so horrible and such a bad influence on Papa."

"If I could risk being a pirate I can certainly risk

being an English planter," the *Comte* said. "It is entirely up to you. But if, my lovely one, you would rather go back to St. Martin, I will agree."

Grania smiled.

"To sell your precious treasures?" she asked. "Of course not! We must stay here, and because you are so brilliant I am quite certain we shall never be found out. Besides, there is no O'Kerry to accuse you of usurping his title."

The *Comte* bent forward and kissed her.

"Then it shall be as you wish," he said, "and you can choose, my darling, in the future as to whether you are a Countess or a *Comtesse* and match the colour of your hair to your choice!"

Grania laughed. Then she called Abe.

"Listen, Abe," she said. "You and only you will know that the gentleman here is really a Frenchman. I expect you heard what the Colonel said."

"I listen, Lady," Abe replied. "Very good news! We be rich. Everyone happy!"

"Of course we will be," Grania said.

"One bit bad news, Lady."

"What is that?" Grania asked.

"New Governor take Momma Mabel. Give big money. Her gone St. George's!"

Grania laughed.

"That means there will be no embarrassment in asking Henri to take over the kitchen."

Her voice rose excitedly as she said:

"Go quickly to the ship, Abe, and ask Henri to come and prepare luncheon. Tell everybody else to come here too, and 'His Lordship' will tell them what has been decided."

She laughed again as she gave the *Comte* his new title.

Then as Abe without saying anything ran from the Drawing-Room and down the steps of the verandah and across the garden, the *Comte* put out his arms and drew her close to him.

"I suppose you know what you are taking on," he

said. "You are going to have to work very hard, my darling, and so shall I."

"But it will be exciting to work together," Grania said, "and I have thought of a new name for you—an English name."

The *Comte* raised his eye-brows as she said:

"I shall call you 'Beau' on English soil, and 'Beaufort' on French. After all, 'Beau' can be applied to Englishmen like Beau Nash, and who could look the part better?"

"As long as that is how I appear to you, then I am satisfied."

He drew her closer still as he added very quietly:

"How can we be so lucky or so blessed as to find a place where we can work and I can make love to you until we can go home?"

"Suppose when the time comes I want to stay here?" Grania asked.

He looked at her to see if she was serious, then realised she was teasing.

His lips were very close to hers as he said:

"Let me make it quite clear once and for all that where I go you will go. You belong to me! You are mine, and not all the nations in the world could divide us or prevent us from being together."

"Oh, darling, that is what I want you to say!" Grania sighed. "And you know I love you."

"I will make you sure of it every day, every hour that we are together," the *Comte* said.

He pulled her almost roughly closer to him.

Then he was kissing her and she knew that once again he was proving his supremacy and domination over her.

It made her adore him because he was so much a man, but at the same time so sensitive and understanding to her feelings.

She knew that with him she would always feel safe and protected. It would not matter where they were, on what island or what part of the world.

His arms were a secret harbour which kept her safe, a harbour that was made of love.

Then as the *Comte*'s kisses grew more demanding she turned her face up to his to say, and her voice trembled:

"Darling, the others will come in a minute. Please do not excite me until . . . tonight."

She saw the fire in the *Comte*'s eyes, but he was smiling.

"Tonight?" he enquired. "Why should we wait until tonight? After luncheon there will be a *siesta*, and I intend to tell you, my wonderful, brave, courageous little wife, how I fell in love with a painting, but fate brought me the reality and she is the most exciting thing I have ever known."

Then he was kissing her again, kissing her until they heard the sound of voices coming from the garden.

It was the sound of men talking excitedly in a language which was not their own.

But to Grania and the *Comte* there was only one language they both understood and which was the same wherever they might be—the language of love.

* * *

The sun-blinds were down and the room, which smelt of jasmine, was very dim. On the lace-edged pillows two heads were very close together.

"*Je t'adore, ma petite,*" the *Comte* said hoarsely.

"I love you . . . I love you, darling."

"Tell me again, I want to be sure."

"I adore . . . you."

"As I adore and worship you, but I also want to excite you."

"How can I . . . tell . . . what I . . . feel?"

Grania's voice was low and breathless. The *Comte*'s hands were touching her and she knew his heart was beating as frantically as hers.

"*Je te desire, ma cherie, je te desire!*"

"And I . . . want you . . . O wonderful, marvellous, Beau . . . love me."

"Give me yourself."

"I am . . . yours . . . yours . . ."

"You are mine, all mine, now and forever."

Then there was only love in a secret harbour which was theirs alone and where no-one else could encroach.

ABOUT THE AUTHOR

BARBARA CARTLAND, the world's most famous romantic novelist, who is also an historian, playwright, lecturer, political speaker and television personality, has now written over 300 books.

She has also had many historical works published and has written four autobiographies as well as the biographies of her mother and that of her brother Ronald Cartland, who was the first Member of Parliament to be killed in W.W. II. This book has a preface by Sir Winston Churchill and has just been republished with an introduction by Sir Arthur Bryant.

Barbara Cartland has sold 200 million books over the world, more than half of these in the U.S.A. She broke the world record in 1975 by writing 23 books and the four subsequent years with 20, 21, 23 and 24. In addition her album of love songs has just been published, sung with the Royal Philharmonic Orchestra.

Barbara Cartland, who is a Dame of the Order of St. John of Jerusalem has championed the cause for old people and founded the first Romany Gypsy Camp in the world.

Barbara Cartland is deeply interested in Vitamin Therapy and is President of the British National Association for Health. Her book the *Magic of Honey* has sold in millions all over the world.

She has a magazine *The World of Romance* and her Barbara Cartland Romantic World Tours will, in conjunction with British Airways, carry travelers to England, Egypt, India, France, Germany and Turkey.